THE WILD, WEIRD WORLDS OF JOHN SLADEK

John Sladek is one of the most exciting new talents to have emerged in the world of science fiction during the past decade. Critics have compared his work with that of Kurt Vonnegut Jr, and with such brilliant *tours-de-force* as *The Müller-Fokker Effect*[1] and *The Reproductive System* he has established a reputation as one of the leading writers of satirical offbeat SF. In this outstanding collection, the reader will encounter wayward time travellers, flying books, computers and robots with scant regard for the Three Laws, and many more disturbing entities—some of them human (all too human,) some alien, some mechanical and some of dubious parentage. In addition, the author has included ten delightful parodies of the work of some of the most highly-regarded names in science fiction.

[1] Also available in Panther Science Fiction.

Also by John Sladek in Panther Science Fiction

The Müller-Fokker Effect

John Sladek

The Steam-Driven Boy

and other strangers

Panther

Granada Publishing Limited
First published in Great Britain in 1973 by Panther Books Ltd
Frogmore, St Albans, Herts AL2 2NF

Acknowledgements

The Secret of the Old Custard first appeared in *IF*, 1966.
The Aggressor first appeared in *Amazing Stories*, 1969.
The Best-Seller first appeared in *Strange Faeces*, 1966.
Is There Death on Other Planets? first appeared in *Ellery Queen's Mystery Magazine*, 1966.
The Happy Breed first appeared in *Dangerous Visions*, 1967 (copyright © Harlan Ellison 1967.)
A Report on the Migrations of Educational Materials first appeared in *The Magazine of Fantasy and Science Fiction*, 1968.
The Singular Visitor from Not-Yet first appeared in *Playboy*, 1968.
The Short, Happy Wife of Mansard Eliot first appeared in *New Worlds Quarterly*, 1971.
The Momster first appeared in *Fantastic*, 1969.
1937 A.D.! first appeared in *New Worlds*, 1967.
Pemberly's Start-Afresh Calliope first appeared in *New World's Quarterly*, 1971.
The Sublimation World first appeared in *The Magazine of Fantasy and Science Fiction*, 1969.

Made and printed in Great Britain by
Richard Clay (The Chaucer Press), Ltd.,
Bungay, Suffolk
Set in Linotype Plantin

CONTENTS

The Secret of the Old Custard

Agnes had been wishing for a baby all day, so it was no surprise to her when she peeked through the glass door of the oven and found one. Bundled in clean flannel, it slept on the wire rack while she scrubbed out dusty bottles, fixed formula and dragged down the crib from the attic. By the time Glen came home from work, she was giving the baby its first bottle.

'Look!' she exclaimed. 'A baby!'

'O my God, where did you get that?' he said, his healthy pink face going white. 'You know it's illegal to have babies.'

'I found it. Why illegal?'

'Everything is illegal,' he whispered, parting the curtains cautiously to peer out. 'Damn near.' The face upon Glen's big, pink, cubical head looked somewhat drawn.

'What's the matter?'

'Oh, nothing,' he said testily. 'We're going to have a gas war, that's all.'

Glen was a pathetic figure as he moved so as not to cast a shadow on the curtains. His bright, skin-tight plastic suit was far from skin-tight, and even his cape looked baggy.

'Is it? Is that all?'

'No. Say, that neighbor of ours has been raking leaves an awfully long time.'

'Answer me. What's wrong? Something at the office?'

'Everything. The carbon paper and stamps and paper clips have begun to disappear. I'm afraid they'll blame me. The boss is going to buy a computer to keep track of the loss. Someone stole my ration book on the train, and I found I had last week's newspaper. I.B.M stock is falling, faintly falling. I have a cold, or something. And—and they're doing away with the Dewey Decimal System.'

'You're just overwrought. Why don't you just sit down and dandle our new baby on your knee, while I rustle up some supper.'

'Stealing food! It's indecent!'

'Everyone does it, dear. Did you know I found the baby in the oven?'

'No!'

'Yes, the queerest thing. I had just been wishing for a baby, and there it was.'

'How are the other appliances doing?'

'The automatic washer tried to devour me. The dishwasher is fading away; we must have missed a payment.'

'Yes, and we're overdrawn,' he said, sighing.

'The garbage disposal is hulking.'

'Hulking?'

'Over there.'

He did not look where she was pointing. He continued to peer out the window, where the weather situation was building up. A Welcome Wagon moved slowly down the street. He could not read the sign, but he recognized the armor plating and the blue snouts of machine-guns.

'Yes, it just sits there hulking in the sink, and it won't eat anything. It ate its guarantee, though.'

The neighbor, a 'Mr Green', paused in his raking to note down the Welcome Wagon's license number.

'Not hulking, darling. *Sulking*.' Glen said.

'You have such a big vocabulary. And you don't even read "How to Build Big Words".'

'I read *Existential Digest*, when I find the time,' he confessed. 'But last week I took their test and learned that I'm not alienated enough. That's why I'm so damned proud of our kids.'

'Jenny and Peter?'

'The same.'

Agnes sighed. 'I'd like to read a copy of the *Irish Mail* some time. By the way, the potatoes had poison again. Every eye.' She went into the bedroom and laid the baby in its crib.

'I'm going down and turn something on the lathe,' Glen announced. 'Something good.'

'Take off your cape first. You remember the safety laws we

learned at P.T.A.'

'Lord, how could I forget? Snuff out all candles. Never stand in a canoe or bathtub. Give name, rank and serial number only. Accept checks only if endorsed in your presence. Do not allow rats to chew on matches, should they so desire.'

He disappeared, and at the same time, Jenny and Peter came home from school, demanding a 'snack'. Agnes gave them Hungarian goulash, bread and butter, coffee and apple pie. They paid 95¢ each, and each tipped her 15¢. They were gruff, dour eight-year-olds who talked little while they ate. Agnes was a little afraid of them. After their snack, they belted on guns and went out to hunt other children, before it grew too dark to see them.

Agnes sighed and sat down to her secret transmitter.

'AUNT ROSE EXPECTED BY NOON TRAIN,' she sent. 'HAVE MADE ARRGTS FOR HER GLADIOLI. SEE THAT FUDGE MEETS 0400 PARIS PLANE WITH CANDLES. THE GARDNER NEEDS TROWEL XPRESS.'

In a moment, the reply came. 'TROWEL ARRGD. FUDGE HAS NO REPEAT NO CANDLES. WILL USE DDT. HOLD ROSE TILL VIOLET HEARD FROM.'

Always the same, tired, meaningless messages. Agnes hid her transmitter in the cookie jar as Glen came up the stairs. He had his own transmitter in the basement, she was sure of that. For all she could tell, it was him she was calling each evening.

'Look at this!' he said proudly, and displayed a newel post.

Outside, a plane dropped leaflets. The neighbor rushed about, raking them up and burning them.

'Every night, the same damned thing,' said Glen, grinding his teeth. 'Every night they drop leaflets telling us to give up, and every night that bastard burns them all. At this rate, we'll never even learn who "they" are.'

'Is it really so important?' she asked. He would not answer. 'Come on, quit hulking. I'll tell you what I want to do. I want to ride on a realway train.'

'*Rail*way,' he corrected. 'You can't, the Public Health Department says that going more than thirty miles an hour contributes significantly to cancer.'

'A lot you care what happens to me!'

Glen bowed his great cube of a head resignedly over the television set. 'You'll notice,' he said, 'that it looks like an innocent Army–Navy football game. And so it may be. Perhaps the ball won't blow up when he kicks it. Perhaps that series of plays is only a coincidence.'

'Number twenty-seven fades back to pass,' she murmured. 'What would that mean, I wonder?'

Glen felt her hand reach out to touch his. He held hands with his wife in the darkened living-room, after making sure she was not wearing her poison ring.

'The common cold,' he muttered. '*They* call it the "common cold". By the way, have I told you we're overdrawn?'

'Yes. It's that damned car. You would have to order all those special features.'

'The bazooka in the trunk? The direction-finder radio? The gun turret? Everyone else had had them for year, Agnes. What am I supposed to do if the police start chasing me? Try to outrun them, me with all that armor plate weighing me down?'

'I just don't see what we're going to live on,' she said.

'We can eat green stamps until——'

'No, they confiscated them this morning. I forgot to tell you.'

The children trooped in, smelling of mud and cordite. Jenny had scratched her knee on a barbed-wire barrier. Agnes applied a bandaid to it, and gave them coffee and doughnuts, 15¢. Then she sent them upstairs to brush their teeth.

'And don't, for God's sake, use the tap water,' Glen shouted. 'There's something in it.' He walked into the room where the baby slept and returned in a minute, shaking his head. 'Could have sworn I heard him ticking.'

'Oh, Glen, let's get away for a few days. Let's go to the country.'

'Oh sure. Travel twenty miles over mined roads to look at a couple of cowpies. You wouldn't dare get out of the car, for fear of the deadly snakes. And they've sowed the ground with poison ivy and giant viruses.'

'I wouldn't care! Just a breath of fresh air——'

'Sure. Nerve gas. Mustard gas. Tear gas. *Pollen.* Even if we survived, we'd be arrested. No one ever goes into the country any more but dope peddlers, looking for wild tobacco.'

Agnes began to cry. Everyone was someone else. No one was who they were. The garbageman scrutinized her messages to the milkman. In the park, the pigeons all wore metal capsules taped to their legs. There were cowpies in the country, but no cows. Even at the supermarket you had to be careful. If you picked out items that seemed to form any sort of pattern . . .

'Are there any popsicles left?' Glen asked.

'No. There's nothing in the icebox but some leftover custard. We can't eat that, it has a map in it. Glen, what *are* we going to eat?'

'I don't know. How about . . . the baby? Well, don't look at me like that! You found him in the oven, didn't you? Suppose you'd just lit the oven without looking inside?'

'No! I will not give up my baby for a—casserole!'

'All right, all right! I was merely making a suggestion, that's all.'

It was dark now, throughout the lead-walled house, except in the kitchen. Out the quartz picture window, dusk was falling on the lawn, on the lifeless body of 'Mr Green'. The television showed a panel discussion of eminent doctors, who wondered if eating were not the major cause of insanity.

Agnes went to answer the front door, while Glen went back to the kitchen.

'Excuse me,' the priest said to Agnes. 'I'm on a sick call. Someone was good enough to loan me his Diaper Service truck, but I'm afraid it has broken down. I wonder if I might use your phone?'

'Certainly, Father. It's bugged, of course.'

'Of course.'

She stood aside to let him pass, and just then Glen shouted, 'The baby! He's at the custard!'

Agnes and the priest dashed out to see. In the clean, well-lighted kitchen, Glen stood gaping at the open refrigerator.

Somehow the baby had got it open, for now Agnes could see his diapered bottom and pink toes sticking out from a lower shelf.

'He's hungry,' she said.

'Take another look,' grated Glen.

Leaning closer she saw the child had pulled the map from the custard. He was taking photos of it with a tiny, baby-sized camera.

'Microfilm!' she gasped.

'Who are you?' Glen asked the priest.

'I'm——'

'Wait a minute. You don't look like a man of the cloth to me.'

It was true, Agnes saw in the light. The breeze rustled the carbon-paper cassock, and she saw it was held together with paper clips. His stole was, on closer examination, a strip of purple stamps.

'If you're a priest,' Glen continued, 'why do I see on your Roman collar *the letterhead of my office*?'

'Very clever of you,' said the man, drawing a pistol from his sleeve. 'I'm sorry you saw through our little ruse. Sorry for you, that is.'

'Our?' Glen looked at the baby. 'Hold on. Agnes, what kind of a vehicle did he drive up in?'

'A diaper truck.'

'Aha! I've been waiting a long time to catch up with you—Diaper Man. Your chequered career has gone on far too long.'

'Ah, so you've recognized me and my dimple-kneed assistant, have you? But I'm afraid it won't do you much good. You see, we already have the photos, and there is a bullet here for each of you. Don't try to stop us!'

Watching them, the false priest scooped up the baby. 'I think I had better kill the two of you in any case,' he said. 'You already know too much about my *modus operandi.*' The baby in his arms waved the camera gleefully and gooed its derision.

'All right,' said Diaper Man. 'Face the wall, please.'

'Now!' said Glen. He leaped for the gun, while Agnes deftly kicked the camera from the baby's chubby fist.

The infant spy looked startled, but he acted fast, a tiny blur of motion. Scooping up two fistfuls of custard, he flung them in Glen's eyes. Gasping, Glen dropped the gun, as the infamous pair made their dash for freedom.

'You'll never take me alive!' snarled the false priest, vaulting into his truck.

'Let them go,' said Glen. He tasted the custard. 'I should have realized earlier the baby wasn't ticking, he was *clicking*. But let them go; they won't get far anyway, and we've saved the map. For whatever it's worth.'

'Are you all right, darling?'

'Fine. Mmmm. This is pretty good, Agnes.'

She blushed at the compliment. There was a muffled explosion, and in the distance they could see flames shooting high in the air.

'Esso bombing the Shell station,' said Glen. The gas war had begun.

The Aggressor

They say that G. was once a man of great commerce, head in fact of a large computer corporation most of whose factories were aboard ships. These ships sailed constantly, through ocean after ocean, leaving in their wakes bits of printed circuit board and bright scraps of wire. G. and his corporate image were known everywhere; he wanted for nothing, and yet——

Yet, sitting in his comfortable office overlooking the showrooms and guard dogs, G. was not very happy. Happy, yes, but not very. Everything he saw made him so *tired*: the array of push-buttons, the towers . . .

One day an engineer came to show him the latest secret processes.

'Look here. This funny material *does something* to the circuit. See? The electrons just get so far, and then they disappear?'

G. thought about this for a minute. He ordered an automobile built of the funny material. When it was ready, he climbed in and let it carry him off down the turnpike.

After he had driven just so far, he came to a toll-gate. The new car rolled to a stop. A man in a peculiar uniform stepped from the ticket booth and called out to him.

'Glad you could make it, Mr G.'

'But how did you know my name?'

'Well, I guess about everybody knows you, Mr G. Come on, I'll take you to the Reception Hall.'

As they walked, G. examined the stranger's peculiar uniform. If you looked at it out of the corner of your eye, it might be any bright color. Only if you looked directly at it was it plain and brown.

'Wait here, in here,' said the man, stopping at the door of the Reception Hall. 'The examiners will be ready to see you in a minute.'

'The examiners?'

'Oh yeah. Everyone has to take an examination, you know. I'm sorry we can't make an exception for such a V.I.P. as yourself, but you know the saying: Regulations are made to be kept.'

G. had to wait in the stuffy hall for hours. He inspected the single tattered magazine in the rack, but it was unreadable. For one thing, every page showed the same picture, with a different headline-caption underneath. The headline-captions were all written in foreign languages, apparently a different language for each page. Supposing they were translations of one another, G. leafed through searching for the English version, but there was none. He read:

'SĂNIAG ĂRUOY TUBĂ ESOLĂ OTĂ GĂNIHTON EVAHĂ ĂUOY! ETINGIĂ KROWĂ EHĂT FOĂ SĂREKROW! ELBANIMOBA SIĂ NOITIDOCĂ NAMUHĂ EHĂT!'

The picture showed a flame.

'HAWO GARK FAER JASO HAFT GAHE JAWO HARK GAIG JANI HATE!'

When he looked closer, he could see something like a shriveled monkey in the middle of the flame.

'YIOU HIAVIE NIOTHIINGI TIO LIOSIE BIUTI YIOURI GIAINISI!'

In the background was a curbing. The flame must have been in the middle of some street.

'ERO KFOITR GHKEEN IRW TOS!'

Very near the flame was a kind of box.

'INTABIL UNHABIL UNEABEBAL UNHABIL INUABLAL UNMABIL UNAABAL INNABEBIL UNCABIL INOABAL INNABIL UNDABIL UNIABAL INTABIL UNIABAL INOABAL INNABEBIL UNIABAL INSABEBIL UNAABAL UNBABIL INOABAL UNMABIL UNIABAL INNABIL UNAABAL UNBABIL UNLABIL UNEABAL!'

The monkey looked in a way human, but small and dark.

'HE CUAE IONDTION AN TBOMABLS!'

He wondered if his entire, spectacular life had been leading up to this—to die in a waiting-room, leafing through an irritating magazine.

'TH HMN CNDTN S BMNBL!'

Or if this waiting itself were a part of the test.

'HET MUNAH NOCDTINOI SI BONIMAABEL!'

Anyway, if this was the kind of thing they were filling their magazines with these days—pictures of a monkey which had somehow escaped from its box and caught fire—he was more than happy to remain a busy and ignorant executive with no time to read!

'I BOMB CONDUIT NOISE-NAIL—HAM THEN!'

This headline looked almost English, but it made no more sense than the others. What, for instance, was a 'noise-nail' supposed to be?

'THEROE HEROUMEROAN CEROONERODEROITIEROON ISERO ABEROOMEROINEROABEROLEROE!'

He threw the magazine down in disgust, just as the four examiners walked into the room.

They introduced themselves as Stone, Brown, White and another whose name G. did not catch. The four looked so much alike, wearing identical drab suits and regimental ties, that G. was never quite sure which one was speaking to him.

'You have three tests to take,' one said. 'Naturally you may fail the first two, but the third is as we say ultra-important. If you fail that you've had it. All clear?'

G. nodded. 'When do I start?'

'Right away. We'll just take you to the Test Center.'

Outside there was just one winding, dusty road leading past the Reception Hall. Not far away stood a series of red signs with white lettering. G. could just make out the first two:

'BEARDS GROW QUICKLY
IN THE GRAVE'

He hoped to read the rest, but the examiners led him off in the opposite direction.

Now that he had a chance to look at them, G. saw the four were also similar in feature and physique. They were heavy, thick-waisted men, with flat noses and facial scars, and the twisted tissue made them seem to smile ironically, the way an old boxer smiles as he holds the bucket for a young boxer to spit in. It was with this cynical smile that one of them pointed at a distant spire. 'I'm hungry,' he said.

They began to climb along a ridge, and G.'s attention was caught by a small lake far below. It was almost covered with what looked like low-flying clouds or enormous suds.

At the sharpest part of the curve, they saw a break in the white guard rail. A vehicle lay on the hillside below them, overturned and in flames. G. stopped for a moment to look, then hurried to catch up with the others.

'Shouldn't we do something?' he asked.

'Too late!' shouted the first examiner, turning a neat handspring.

'Happens all the time!' bellowed the second, flinging himself into a triplet of somersaults.

The third ripped off his belt and began skipping rope without breaking his stride. 'They never learn!' he screamed.

'What do they think a guard rail is for, anyway—decoration?' boomed the last, leaping into the air to do a lightning-fast *entrechat*.

While wondering at his companions' lack of compassion, G. was no grumbler; he plodded on. Presently one of them shouted, 'There's the Test Center!'

The others grinned at one another, and one of them, nudging G., said, 'Isn't the air beautiful?'

It did seem a question, and G. was too busy looking over the Test Center to try framing an answer.

The Test Center, as far as he could see, looked exactly like the Reception Hall. Its thick, concrete-block walls were windowless. A single elm obscured most of the large sign painted on one side wall: '. . . E! THIS MEANS YOU!'

As they approached the glass doors, a beggar accosted them. His smile, as he hold out a *fasces* of pencils, was even more scar-twisted and cynical than those of the examiners. His suit, too, was a frayed copy of theirs, and around his shirtless throat was an oily regimental tie.

'Pencils, boss?'

One of the examiners hit him hard, in the mouth and stomach, then moved courteously to open the door for G.

'That's the kind of thing we came along to protect you from,' he said. G. raised his eyebrows, but could think of no reply. For just a second, he longed to be once more in his own cool corridors, among the clean young systems analysts.

The examiners showed him to a soundproof cubicle and explained the three tests:

'You just type your answers on that there keyboard, see?'

'And the computer asks you more question.'

'The first two tests are a kind of warmup...'

'...then the computer gives you the real battle problem.'

'Good luck, now.'

They left him alone with the computer typewriter, which at once asked him the first question:

'C GAVE B AS MANY TIMES AS MANY APPLES AS A HAD AS B NOW GIVES C OF HIS OWN APPLES. C GAVE A ENOUGH APPLES TO MAKE A'S TOTAL 5 TIMES WHAT B ORIGINALLY HAD. WHEN C HAD EATEN ENOUGH OF HIS OWN APPLES TO LEAVE HIM 2/3 OF WHAT A NOW HAS, HE HAD LOST ALTOGETHER 4 TIMES AS MANY APPLES AS HE GAVE A. A NOW GIVES C 1/7 OF HIS APPLES, AND C BUYS AS MANY MORE AS HE GAVE B, THUS DOUBLING HIS TOTAL SUPPLY. A WILL GIVE B 1 MORE APPLE THAN C WILL GIVE B. IF B EATS 2 APPLES, HE WILL THEN HAVE 5 TIMES AS MANY APPLES AS A NOW GIVES HIM. A WILL FINALLY HAVE 1 LESS APPLE THAN C NOW HAS, AND C WILL FINALLY HAVE 1/2 AS MANY APPLES AS HE HAD ORIGINALLY. B NOW HAS 1/2 AS MANY APPLES AS C HAD AFTER HE GAVE B AS MANY APPLES AS A WILL GIVE B. C NOW HAS 4 TIMES AS MANY APPLES AS THERE ARE MONTHS REMAINING IN THE YEAR. WHAT MONTH IS IT?'

G. answered or failed to answer, and the second question came:

'ASSUMING THEM TO BE "SUSPENSIONS" OF ONE ART MEDIUM IN ANOTHER, LIST THE FOLLOWING SIX WORKS IN ORDER OF IMPORTANCE, CATEGORIZING THEM BY *DEGREE* OF SUSPENSION, AND DISCUSSING THE *TYPE* OF SUSPENSION, WHETHER ANALOGICALLY "COLLIDAL" OR OTHERWISE, HOW MUCH OF EACH MEDIUM HAS GONE INTO SUSPENSION, ETC.

'1. O. FLAKE, "DER ZELTWEG"

'2. J. ASHBY, "DESIGN FOR A BRAIN"

'3. CLYDE OHIO, "EXTENSION"

'4. R. MUTT, "FOUNTAIN"

'5. J. C. ODEON, "O"

'6. L. POSTMAN AND R. D. WALK, "PERCEPTION OF ERROR"'

When G. had made an attempt at answering this, there came a third:

'A PRIEST AND THREE NUNS ARE SHIPWRECKED ON A DESERT ISLAND WITH NO HOPE OF RESCUE. FOOD IS RUNNING LOW, AND UNTIL THEY CAN RAISE SOME CROPS, THERE IS SERIOUS DANGER OF STARVATION. IN AN ACCIDENT, THE PRIEST LOSES BOTH ARMS. HE IS BARELY SAVED, BUT A DILEMMA ARISES: WHETHER OR NOT THE FOUR MAY EAT HIS SEVERED ARMS, INCLUDING OR EXCLUDING THE CONSECRATED FOREFINGERS AND THUMBS.

'WITHOUT HIS HELP, FARMING GOES SLOWLY. IT IS CLEAR THAT IN A FEW YEARS THEY MAY ALL STARVE TO DEATH, UNLESS THEY BREAK THEIR VOWS OF CHASTITY AND PROCREATE.

'THE PRIEST HAS A DREAM IN WHICH WHAT HE SUPPOSES TO BE AN ANGELIC MESSENGER APPEARS, BATTERED AND BLOODSTAINED, TO INFORM HIM THAT THE DEVIL HAS TEMPORARILY TAKEN CONTROL OF HEAVEN AND REIGNS SUPREME. WHOEVER DOES NOT IMMEDIATELY RENDER WORSHIP TO SATAN WILL BE CAST INTO HELL. "IT IS ONLY TEMPORARY," THE ANGEL STRESSES. "I'M SURE THE LORD HAD SOME REASON FOR ALLOWING THIS TO TAKE PLACE."

'SOLVE THESE DILEMMAS.'

For the second test, the computer opened up to show G. a passage down into the earth. He followed it to a room containing three appliances: an automatic washer, a garbage disposal and a television set. As printed placards directed him, he took off his shirt and tie and put them into, respectively, the washer and the disposal. The shirt was torn to threads instantly, and though he managed to retrieve the tie, it was wrinkled and covered with grease. He managed to knot it correctly nevertheless.

The television flickered at him a series of stills of famous actresses, which G. correctly identified as Carole Lombard, Gene Tierney, Marilyn Monroe, Jayne Mansfield. Their eyes seemed to follow him wherever he walked in the room. After several repeats of the series, the words, 'PROCEED TO NEXT ROOM' appeared on the screen. G. obeyed.

He was in the waiting-room of a large air terminal, standing before Gate I. Suddenly a crowd of people came running out of Gate I and knocked him down. No one stopped to see if he were hurt; the entire mob rushed over to Gate III and disappeared. G. had barely time to get to one knee (and examine the other, which was bleeding) when a second group galloped out of Gate II, swinging infants and suitcases. He had time to see how pleasantly ordinary they were—neat computer programmers, jolly tourists, old folks, women in print dresses and men in straw shoes, attaché cases, cameras, zip bags of dirty diapers—before they ran him down.

These hurried to Gate IV, leaving G. with a cut lip, a torn lapel and scraps of animated conversation:

'... on a non-sked ... bonded and ... potty ... Did you *see* that chicken sandwich?'

There was no time for G. to get out of the way. He was run over and trampled in quick succession by passengers bound from Gates III to I, IV to II, I to II, II to I, III to II, IV to III, I to IV, II to III, III to IV and IV to I. By now, he was barely able to crawl into the next room, a barracks.

The soldiers wearing Aggressor army fatigues and cockscomb helmets saw him and roared out oaths in Esperanto. They trussed G. to a ladder and began hacking bits from him and toasting them over cigarette lighters. Yet even through his intense pain, G. knew all this would end happily; he didn't mind the torture as much as not being allowed to smoke.

A bell rang. The soldiers hurriedly took off their Aggressor uniforms and put on Army green. They 'discovered' G. still strapped to a ladder and released him. Was he all right? they wanted to know. One soldier bet him it had been hell, being a prisoner of the inhuman Aggressor. G. smiled and shrugged, and asked if anyone had a cigarette, preferably filtered. No one smoked, and though one sergeant offered him a chocolate bar, G. felt badly treated. He was weary and restless at the same time; he would have liked to do anything ... sell pencils, anything ...

As a veteran, G. was taken to lead the parade past his own suburban home. Joan, his wife, waved at him from the front yard, which needed a bit of trimming. She had changed her hair style he noted, giving an extra grin to her hair. It looked nice, at least from a distance. *He waved, and she waved back,* he thought. *They were like that—casual, you know?*

The street was lined with neat programmers and systems analysts, who showered him with the punchings from punched cards.

'Thanks, boys. Back to work now.'

At the end of the street was the square red can. When he saw it, G. knew what he must do to pass the test. Somewhere in the background, four-foot, up-to-the-minute-news letters spelled out the computer's problem:

'THEY SAY THAT G. WAS A MAN OF GREAT COMMERCE, HEAD IN FACT OF A LARGE COMPUTER CORPORATION ...'

The crowds watched this news with solemn interest, but when it caught up with the present, they broke into cheers.

'... IT WROTE, AND THEN G. TOOK UP THE CAN AND POURED THE GASOLINE OVER HIMSELF. HE ASKED A NEARBY GENERAL FOR A LIGHT, AND THOUGH THE GENERAL WAS A NONSMOKER HIMSELF, HE WAS A GENTLEMAN. HIS BUTANE LIGHTER WORKED ON THE FIRST TRY.

'G. MADE A LOVELY FLAME, EVEN IN BLACK AND WHITE,' it wrote, and then G. took up the can ...

The Best-Seller

A synopsis

Book One: *Adrian*

Four couples gather at a small seaside hotel for a summer vacation. The hotel is located on an island connected to the mainland by a bridge. On the morning of their arrival, the bridge is washed away by a storm, and they are stranded.

All of them have read the Decameron, and the time is heavy upon them. Instead of relating tales, they elect to make up stories—perhaps true, perhaps not—about the eight of them and their relationships. One person will be delegated each day to chronicle the day's events, embellish them in any way he pleases and read them in the evening to his companions.

Adrian Warner, the architect, draws the first day. He writes in a blunt, honest manner, such as might be expected from a worker in concrete.

He begins with an account of how his wife, Etta, falls in love with another guest, the ruthless young steel executive, Farmer Bill. Caught by the morning storm, these two take shelter in a cave on the beach. Bill returns her caresses but not her love. Though she is beautiful, Farmer Bill despises her as he despises his wife, Theda, a dark-eyed beauty who is also the only brewmistress on this continent. He loves only Glinda Cook, a thin, pale Southern girl with a dreamy manner, mouse-brown hair and crooked teeth.

Glinda is not, it is true, happy with her husband, Van Cook the popular columnist. But if anyone is captain of her heart, it is the effeminate, smirking hagiographer, Dick Hand.

That evening at dinner, Van Cook recklessly declares that he loves Mrs Hand, and challenges Dick to a duel. Dick laughingly suggests water pistols of ink and bathing suits.

'Done!' Cook cries fiercely.

The duel takes place on the hotel terrace after dinner. Far down the beach can be heard the plaintive notes of Etta's English horn (a professional musician, she has wandered off by herself to practice). Each of the combatants is given a water pistol loaded with ink the same color as his own bathing trunks: Cook has red, Hand has washable black. The winner is to be decided by Dolly Hand, a large, raw-boned woman of fifty, said to have once been a drum majorette. Dolly seems utterly uninterested.

Cook fouls intentionally, clinching and squirting red ink in Hand's eyes. Dick is somewhat of a coward, and fails to score a hit on his opponent. After a few futile sallies, he contents himself with squirting his ink at Adrian, who is attired in a white dinner jacket. Hand makes several such passes before timekeeper Glinda calls a halt.

When the fight is over, Cook's fouling becomes evident. He has been hitting in the clinches, and the red ink until now has hidden the blood. Glinda begins to tenderly wipe Dick's battered face, but he pulls away from her and, giggling, squirts more black ink at Adrian. The architect, angry, leaps to his feet.

'See here now!' he cries. Then his face grows ashen as he looks down at the black stain on his jacket.

The others demand to know who won—but Dolly, the referee, cannot be found! She has slipped away during the fight, and someone reports seeing her white-booted figure dragging another woman away down the beach. The sound of Etta's horn has stopped.

The stains on Adrian's jacket form letters, spelling 'I LOVE Y'.

Book Two: *Theda*

In his langourous and elliptic style, the sloe-eyed brewmaster reveals that all that has gone before is a lie. Adrian Warner is a bitch and a liar. She has lied about the sex of everyone.

First of all it is she, not her husband Etta, who loves the lady foundry exec, Farmer Bill. Yesterday Adrian pretended affection for him, Theda, only until she persuaded him to fall for her. But today, as Theda puts it, the truth outs.

Passing the grape arbor this morning, on his way to the

summer house, Theda hears Adrian confess her love for Farmer. Bill. Bill rejects this love, declaring in turn that she loves only the manly Etta. Yesterday Etta seemed to love her too, but today, since his night with Dolly on the beach, Etta seems oddly distracted.

Theda is in a hopelessly false position now, sick with love for a confirmed lesbian. Another surprise awaits him as he enters the summer house. Someone throws arms about Theda and kisses him roughly—it is Etta!

'Careful you don't ruin your lip,' says Theda, squirming away. Etta laughs heartily at his ignorance of music. Confessing that he has been converted the previous night from heterosexuality by Dolly, Etta invites Theda to spend tonight alone on the beach. Sickened, the brewmaster refuses.

Coquettish Van Cook still pursues Dolly, but the big drum major kicks her in the eye at lunch. He appears to flirt instead with her husband, Glinda, a shy Southern boy. Glinda passes Dick Hand a note protesting that he still loves her, and chiding her for her silly infatuation with Van Cook. Theda, who delivers the note, asks her about this.

'It's true,' Dick sighs. 'I'm a hagiographress, you know. I've even offered to prove a saint in her ancestry—anything—but she refuses to even speak to me. Sometimes I wish Dolly and I could change sex . . .'

The rest of the day is sultry and oppressive with rage and desire, as they all sit around the hotel lounge. Farmer spends hours scrawling Etta's name on the tablecloth, even drawing his profile. Etta glowers at Theda, and tries to tear up his manuscript. In the ensuing fight, Theda loses an ear, which his opponent eats.

Book Three: *Van*

With all respect to those who have gone before him, the columnist states that both Theda and Adrian have had their reasons for exaggerating some truths, concealing others. Perhaps it is up to a newspaperman, a dealer in facts, to get at some kind of objectivity about this, as he calls it, 'love nest'.

He makes no apology about his passion for Dick Hand, but

let him cast the first stone, etc., for the truth is, there isn't a man or woman among the eight who isn't queer this third day.

The little balding hagiographer, a former goalee for a prominent Canadian hockey team, now loves none but A. Warner. This architect, designer of the well-known Piedmont Tower and famed for his new building principle, the 'concrete truss', remains firm in his attachment to 35-year-old steel magnate Farmer Bill. The ironic quadrangle is complete, for Bill, long supposed an entrenched hetero, has conceived love for the narrator. Farmer Bill came to power through a merger between a steel corporation and the molybdenum trust of which he was co-chairman three years ago. He is now married to the former Theda Baker, and has one child, Ebo.

The women also pursue a hopeless path. Theda loves patient Glinda, a gracious Southern lady with a flair for entertaining, granddaughter of the governor of her state. Glinda married your reporter six years ago. They have no children.

Perhaps for this reason she is drawn to the youthful, robust Dolly Hand, who once danced for a living and can still kick high as a man's eye. Her loves includes spinach, basketball, and Etta Peer Warner, the latter hopelessly. Etta allegedly remains true to her former love, the darkly beautiful, brawny brewmistress.

Although the hotel staff do their best to make everyone as comfortable as possible, they are prisoners and they know it. When, late in the afternoon a plane flies overhead, they all rush out to the beach to wave at it. Passing low, it seems to be flying on out of sight without noticing them. Then as it reaches the mainland, it begins to bank around, coming back for another pass.

Unfortunately it is too low for this manoeuvre. One wing brushes a treetop, and all at once the plane is a mass of flame, pinwheeling along through the forest. It explodes and settles, starting a forest fire on the mainland that rages all night, seen only by helpless witnesses on the island.

Book Four: *Dolly*

'I am a drug addict. Do not pity me. I ask only for your understanding. This illness has been my secret for a long time. Too long...'

Thus begins Dolly's amazing narrative. She gives the background of the persons present: addicts all. Dick, her Dickybird, was once addicted to cocaine stirred into cocoa, though now he lives on reserpine stirred into raspberry brandy.

Etta and Adrian mix thorazine and thiamine, laced with Meretran and Serutan. 'Pothead' Van Cook and Glinda move in a dream of Nembutal and Hadacol, Darvon and Ritalin, while Farmer Bill and Theda have long existed utterly without food, taking in only methedrine and methanol.

And of course Dolly herself. Having tried every drug in the vocabulary, she is currently experimenting, mixing drugs and liqueurs, such as benzedrine/Benedictine, such as dramamine /Drambuie ... The night gets longer.

Why is it, she wonders, that everyone lies? Wish-fulfillment explains some of it. Van Cook pretended Farmer Bill loved him when the opposite was true. But why does he ignore Theda's love for him? How can he ignore her attempted overdose-suicide? Can he keep claiming she just wanted to hog the horse?

Alas! If Theda could only love Glinda, things might be far different. Poor little Glinda, seven months' PG, half blind from Sterno breakfasts, head-over-heels in love with Theda. She even offers to sit with little Ebo, while Theda takes her overdose.

Adrian, after twice being the object of sick Dick's affections, now returns the favor, but too late. Dick has written a poem to his new love, Etta, comparing the sound of her horn to the clash of waves on the seventh level of his consciousness. Etta tries to use him to get at Dolly, who admits feeling only disgust for the little Serutan-head.

Words crowd in upon Dolly here. She never wanted to be an addict; they told her pot would help her march better, as she led the high school band. It was a lie.

Now she leaves her manuscript for a moment to try to caress

Adrian, who is passing in the hall.

Now Adrian's firm hand adds that he has smashed Dolly in the teeth with her steel baton. It is, he adds, manufactured by Farmer Bill's corporation.

Book Five: *Etta*

As only she and her husband know, Etta is an endocrinologist. In clinically precise terms, she details the events of the fifth day.

Food and water are running low, and sanitary facilities are less than adequate. Etta has divided the remainder of the quinine and insect repellant, and rations it strictly. She tries to make do with a crude first-aid kit, treating Theda's ear, Van's eye and the lacerations on Dick's face. Now a clumsy waiter spills *crêpes suzettes* on Farmer Bill's lap, inflicting second-degree burns. Then there is Dolly's mouth requiring dental tools Etta does not have, and Ebo develops diaper rash.

Moving about only before or after the midday heat, the men gather firewood for nightfall, as well as a few straight boards for splints. The women tear up sheets for bandages. It becomes increasingly hard to sterilize everything, especially in time to deliver Glinda's stillborn child, but by working night and day, Etta manages somehow, and somehow manages to keep up her journal, too. Glinda is very weak and very ill. Only the hope of Theda's returning her pitiful love keeps her alive. Etta makes Theda be nice to Glinda.

What a strange thing a woman's friendship is, Etta thinks. Like the love of a leopard, it is wild, shy and a little hurtful. She means not only Glinda's love for Theda but her own love for Dolly, who seems to be, poor silly bitch, in love with her own husband.

But are the males less fickle? Today Adrian spurns the love of Dick Hand as resolutely as yesterday he sought it. Dick chases him from copse to copse as they gather fuel. Adrian expresses his concern about Glinda.

'I don't care whose child it is,' he says hoarsly. 'I'll marry her, if she'll have me.'

But Glinda loves Theda, who loves her husband Farmer

Bill fiercely. Now Farmer Bill brings in Van Cook, who has collapsed with sunstroke, and there is a new tenderness in the industrialist's eye as he gazes on the stricken man. Ah, what strange things are our endocrines!

Van Cook whispers in his delirium one name over and over: 'Etta!'

Book Six: *Farmer*

In tough, short sentences, Bill spells it out. He loves Etta. No one else. Others may have time to mess around. Not Bill. He knows what he wants, now, after a lifetime of banging around from one job to another. He wants to paint.

Some say it takes guts to do this, to scrap your life and start all over. It doesn't. A man does what he has to do, that's all. Bill has to paint.

It's like breathing. From the chest. Where the heart is. If a man goes wrong, he might as well rip out his heart and smash it. Bill paints, and it's right.

He wants to paint Etta nude, maybe in fresco ten stories high, the way he feels about her. What she has doesn't need a name.

But Etta has a lesbo hang-up with the Southern girl, Gilda, who is mooning over Dolly the Dyke. It's enough to make a real man puke.

Doll is meanwhile gone on her own freaky husband, tricky Dicky. But he as usual has eyes for a man, Van Cook. If you can call him a man, the way he simpers at Adrian Warner.

At least Adrian has real balls. He's hung on Theda, your narrator's wife. The original castrating bitch. She'd like to castrate Bill, and keep him from painting. So he couldn't paint Etta nude. Theda admits as much.

She admits loving Bill.

Book Seven: *Glinda-girl.*

Because it don't matter what Her sisters thought of Her that time in Billy Framer's dirty-green roadster out back of the feed sump, everyone seems like they're dying and the afternoon's so still you could hear the town bumblebee clear down to the

Metro. At the Rich Hand place they got someone's guts strung out hanging all over a tree at Xmas like firehose because Theda means death you know some folks don't like Cookie what he done to Dolly's nipples with the broken Agri-cola bottle was real mean even if she loves him and what father don't but Cookie's a idiot certified by Doc Sam H. Smith. She wishes it was Rich Hand in that car not Billy though he's a hunchback too he at least has one pretty blue eye like Etta's dress and loafers made of human skin Rich likes Dolly because she's his son, that's why he raped her with the dove-handle.

Because Etta means teat She wishes Her sister Etta had gone ahead and hatched out that baby inside of her so that She could play with it but it was by Adrian, their son from that winter when they were so poor there wasn't nothing to burn in the stove but dried snot Etta wants to be nice and flat for Billy. The rats ate his toes off that same winter and Theda the woman with no jaw she's got hair on her chest Adrian says he should know he's her mother but she wants him for some reason he only liked Theda whipping her with his saw again last winter the Doc took off her arm up to the elbow and Reverend Bregs said to thank God for what's left only this year they took off the rest of it Theda says it's time to stop being thankful she lost it the time Adrian's pig hospital burned to the ground the same night he asked Etta to marry him he still loves her like a brother but she wants Billy to touch her again with his double finger he's all fat and greasy She can see why Etta don't want him no more but Theda does still.

Because She loves Rich Hand even helping him dig his mother's body up to make sure about the rings and something had eaten the fingers She laughed till She split but no one loves Her but Cookie all covered with sores from sand fights and can't move his armpit since the railroad flood he says he never hanged a baby before.

Book Eight: *Dick:* Epilogue.

Much has happened since that fateful vacation. After their rescue these eight characters part and go each his own way in search of a story. Dick Hand keeps track of them, however:

He has stopped loving Dolly and divorced her so that he could be with Adrian. Unable to bear this, Dolly has travelled to the tropics where she witnesses an unusual savage torture, organic crucifixion. She settles on this as her mode of suicide, and employs expert savage torturers to help her. First a *yab-yab*, or needlewood tree of the proper height and shape is selected. Four of its spiny limbs are severed, and and to their stumps the natives securely bind Dolly's hands and feet. In the fast-growing tropics, the limbs mature again in a matter of hours, piercing her extremities. To torture Dick, Dolly records every minutes of her seven-hour agony on the tape, and arranges for it to be mailed to him.

Etta meanwhile has left Adrian and is actually on the train going to live with Dolly when she hears over the radio of the former drum majorette's tragic death. Petrified with horror and grief, Etta descends from the train at once, in the city where by chance Adrian lives.

Adrian has just received a long mash note from Dick, which so depresses him that he goes to the train station, with the half-idea of throwing himself before a train. But he sees Etta and falls in love with her all over again.

It is, alas, too late. In vain does Adrian take Etta to the basement of Piedmont Tower, his architectural triumph, and in vain does he explain the concrete truss. Etta seems like a zombie.

Still she must somehow absorb part of his lecture on super-stressed concrete, the circular cantilever, the 'primum mobile' principle, etc., for later that night she returns to Piedmont Tower alone, with an acetylene torch. The watchman, having seen her in the company of the architect, suspects nothing as he lets her into the basement once again.

There she straps herself to one of the huge concrete beams —so like a bent bow—and cuts through the restraining steel support! The beam straightens suddenly, and as Piedmont Tower splits apart from top to bottom, she is flung one hundred thirty stories into the air—to fall impaled on the United Pin Company's giant sign.

Adrian learns of her death that night. He at once books

passage on the liner *Henkersmahl*, his hold luggage two steamer trunks. One is filled with nitric acid in a delicate glass envelope; the other with plastic explosives, pickled in turpentine. He supervises their loading to make sure they are placed next to each other. The process of loading naturally breaks the glass envelope, and it will take exactly seventy-two hours for the nitric acid to eat its way out through the thick metal of the trunk.

The second night of its voyage, the *Henkersmahl* sends out a call for help. 'Some madman' has poured gasoline into the lifeboats and set them afire. The ship is saved only by casting all lifeboats adrift. Only one ship, the *Vivisectress*, hears the call for help. It is too far away to alter course, just for the loan of a lifeboat or two, though it wishes the *Henkersmahl* well.

The following night a flaming explosion tears out the bottom and sets the ship afire. Blazing oil coats the water all about. The lifejackets are discovered to be soaked with fuel oil. It is suicide to enter the water wearing one.

Adrian seizes the ship's wireless to explain to the world his crime: suicide.

'The cut wrist, the gas oven were not sure enough,' he shouts, over the screams of old people and children. 'We all know how the life-principle thwarts our pitiful suicide attempts. I had to leave myself no escape at all ...'

The transmission ends.

Theda has gone to work in a beauty parlor, where she soon falls into the hands of a vicious lesbian white slave ring. After contributing several articles to men's magazines ('Passion Darlings of the Hell Camp for Lesbians'; 'Chained Virgins for the Half-Beast Women'; 'I Was a Love Slave to the Handmaidens of Horror'; 'I Was Possessed by the Harpies from Hell'; 'TRAPPED!—By Sex-Amazons of the Queen of Slaughter!') she quietly succumbs, dildoed to death in an alley off a fashionable street.

At the other end of the city in the bohemian district lives her husband, Farmer Bill. No longer a foundry executive, he has become a starving frescoist. He loves Glinda, who has long since returned to her birthplace in the South. Now working as a group therapist in an exclusive brothel, Glinda cares only for her dashing husband, Van Cook.

Van, seeking still to impress Theda with his bravery, has quit his newspaper job and become a hot pilot, a cropduster. He limits his writing to a novel about this new life, THE CROPDUSTERS. ('The story of those happy-go-lucky flyboys who daily face death over Nebraska, to combat the Third Horseman, Pestilence. The story of the planes they fly, the lives they live, the women they love.') But this dangerous, manly occupation does not advance him in Theda's favor at all; she loves Farmer Bill. When Van Cook hears of her death, he sends off a suicide telegram to Dick, then crashes his plane, a Mr Mulligan, into the corn.

Glinda, unable to endure life without her man, enters a pie-eating contest in the hope of exploding the walls of her intestines. She does not succeed. Having won the contest by consuming thirty-four apricot pies, she is rushed off to the hospital to have her stomach pumped.

Here kind Fate aids her suicide plan. In this ever-summery Southern city the hospital is located in a veritable forest of honeysuckle, rambling rose and lilac. This summer evening the windows of the pumping room are open for coolness, and the sweet scent drifts in. Glinda is unable to speak, so the attendants assume she is a pill suicide attempt. They strap her down, gag her throat open with a plastic funnel and slide the pump tube down to her stomach. Soon a swarm of honeybees, attracted from their murmurous haunts by the smell of pumped apricots, streams into the room.

Glinda lies helpless as the bees chase her attendants away, then enter this curious red flower, hot on the scent of fetid apricot jam. Her death agonies, Dick speculates in what is for him an unusual moment of subjectivity, must have been excruciating.

When Farmer Bill learns of the death of his beloved, he behaves stoically, determined to transmute his feelings into art. He begins a giant, three-storey fresco called *Gilda*.

Dick explains here that this is *his* suicide note. He cannot go on without Adrian, and so has already made ample preparation for his own death:

Having acquired a considerable fortune through investments in horticultural enterprises, Dick Hand has been able to purchase control of the government of a small African nation. Carefully he sows the seed of revolt here, employing men expert in such matters to (1) rouse the populace to acts of rebellion, and (2) persuade the government to take ever-stricter reprisals (decimations, unbearably heavy taxes, compulsory military service for the aged and unfit, curfews in effect at strange hours of the day, fines for drinking water, etc.).

The head of state, President Rudy Bung, is so terrified of his own people that he is forever incognito, wearing a black stocking over his head and giving his speeches falsetto. Having made sure the revolution will succeed, Dick secretly spirits away Rudy Bung, kills him and assumes his identity. Alone in the presidential office, Dick is killed at once by the insurgents and—as he had hoped and planned—unspeakable things are done to his corpse.

This last story is a news clipping, of course. In the next column is an item about the collapse of a large wall; the frescoist Farmer Bill is crushed under seventy tons of wet plaster.

The End

The above ending was rejected by the publisher as 'too downbeat'. Accordingly the author wrote the following ending, which the publisher accepted:

Book Eight: *Dick:* Epilogue.

Much has happened since that fateful vacation. After their rescue these eight characters part and go each his own way in search of a story. Dick Hand keeps track of them, however:

Adrian and Etta decide to face squarely and together the problem of his drinking. She works as a movie extra to raise the money for his psychiatrist. Adrian is fiddling with a brilliant new design for a bomb shelter, the 'clamshell womb'. It has the unique feature of being located well *above* the blast area, on a tower several miles high. A world-renowned architect, now crippled with age, comes as a humble student to study and admire Adrian's design. Etta gets a starring rôle, which she declines. Being Adrian's wife, she says, is fame enough for any gal!

Glinda and Van Cook are drifting apart, as he gives up his job with the paper and becomes a pilot, seeding clouds. But after all their differences, after the failure of a dozen ministers and marriage counselors, they are at last reunited by the smallest imaginable of marriage counselors, a gentleman only five pounds three ounces in weight—Van Jr. Van begins work on a novel about his work, THE RAINMAKERS. He flies his GeeBee racer seldom and with great care—now that he has so much love to come home to.

Theda has become a beautician, Mr Theda, famous on three continents. She has not seen Bill for seventeen years. One day he comes to the beauty parlor dressed in old clothes, his beard rough, his hair a mess, crushing his old hat in hands with broken nails and cracked cuticles. He wants another chance to prove his love for her. Theda means to order him to leave, but she sees tears in his eyes. The sight makes tears spring to her own, and one of her contact lenses is washed out. As they crawl around looking for it, they touch hands...

Dick finishes by relating his own story. He has become a successful, gruff but kind-hearted dermatologist. Night calls keep him from thinking too much about Dolly, who has entered a hospital to kick her habit. Nine months drag by, and then one Spring day she walks weakly to the gate. There he is, grinning shyly, carrying one of her old batons. They run to embrace one another. She gives her old baton an expert twirl!

'Darling,' he says huskily, 'it's time to go home.'

Is There Death on Other Planets?

I could have gone back to Earth, thought Peter, hurrying through the fog-shrouded evening. I could have hitch-hiked to California and drunk cokes at big, fluorescent-lighted drive-ins.

Under every street light Peter paused, looking back. And always the short man with sunglasses was there. One street light behind him.

The gutters of Centerville, capital of the planet Lumpkin, were littered with every variety of garbage. Up to a few hours ago, Peter thought, I was part of that garbage. And now? Now I am a spy, an agent of the U.S. government.

'Me a spy? Here on Lumpkin? I can't do it! I don't even look like a spy. I'm only a pace bum. Look, my clothes are canvas from a space ship. My belt is a bit of tarred rope.'

The man in the green hat sighed. 'You'll do. As the great *n*-tuple agent Waldmir said, "More than anyone else, a spy must look like anyone else."' The face was invisible beneath the brim of the green hat; Peter saw only a row of jagged lower teeth. 'Now here's the plan: Lumpkin wants war with the U.S., and they're ready to attack. All they need is for their computer to give the word. When the auspices are right, they'll launch enough missiles to turn the United States of Earth into a fireball.

'Your job is to steal the gizmo that programs the computer. It's a small device, easily concealed in this satchel. You're to deliver it at the rocket terminal to a man called Adrian. He'll be wearing a green hat like this, and he runs the postcard concession. Got it?'

'Where do I get it, though? And how?'

'It's locked up in the War Department's safe.' The man handed Peter a package of cigarettes. 'This is in reality a time machine. You'll simply project yourself into the future, watch yourself open the safe, and thus learn the combination. Then you come back into the present and open the safe. Got it?'

'Seems to me there's a paradox there somewhere,' mused Peter, scratching his unshaven chin. 'But go on. What happens after I deliver it?'

'Once we have the gizmo—which closely resembles a rare old phonograph record, they say—we'll be able to re-program their computer. We'll fool it into believing the war is over, and that the U.S. has won. Our troops will land at once, and our army of trained tourists will follow, to punish the rebellious Lumpkinites.' The man ran his tongue over the jagged teeth in a gesture of keen anticipation. 'But you'd better get started. There isn't much time.'

The little man in sunglasses was still behind him. Ahead was a sign: 'ANNIE'S EARTHSIDE BAR. Your home away from home—No Credit.' Gratefully Peter ducked into the ill-lit, evil-smelling taproom. How well he knew this derelict retreat—and its lovely proprietress.

Annie came to his table and leaned over him, her raven hair brushing his cheek. Her slender alabaster throat worked with unspoken emotion, as huskily she breathed, 'No Credit.'

'Annie, you've got to hide me.'

But no, already it was too late! Pressing his package of cigarettes, Peter could see that the little man would find him here. Sighing, he ordered a beer and began telling Annie about the fauna of that exotic planet, Earth.

'Then there's the animal *ghosts*. Like the Bansheep. You're walking alone in Ionia at night, see? Suddenly you hear this awful wail: *Gaaaaa*. You see something big and white moving out there in the darkness——'

'You told me that one,' she said. The short, weasel-faced man came in and sat at the next table. He removed his sunglasses, and Peter saw that his eyes never strayed from the satchel in Peter's hand.

'Then how about the Grisly Bear? That's the blood-dripping spirit of a bear that prowls the forests of Iowa. He can't get back to his body, see, because someone killed it while he was sleeping. Hibernating. He prowls in Ireland——'

'You said Iowa.'

'I meant Ireland, of course. Where all bears' souls go when they are hibernating. That's why they call it Hibernia.'

The little man drew a laser gun, just as Peter knew he would. 'What have you got in that satchel?' he asked, right on cue.

'Only an old phonograph record.' It was a desperate move, but the wrong one.

'Is it the Andrews Sisters, singing "Apple Blossom Time?" If so, then I arrest you in the name of——'

Taking a tighter grip on the satchel, Peter passed out.

He came to his senses in an opulent apartment, where an equally opulent blonde was arguing with the weasel-like man. Waving a saw, the girl exclaimed, 'It's the only way! The satchel is made of some impenetrable material, and he refuses to let go of it.'

'Mmf. You may be right, my dear. But can't we just search him and get the key to the satchel?'

'Search him? Ugh! I refuse to touch that filthy creature,' she replied, giving a ladylike shudder.

'I'm awake!' Peter announced. 'Here, I'll open the case for you.'

'Do not try any tricks, my filthy friend,' the man snarled. 'Roberta, keep him covered with the saw.'

While he pretended to ply the lock, Peter stalled for time. 'Have I ever told you about the Were-hen? In eastern Iceland, when the hen-bane blooms and the Moon looks like a big devilled egg, the peasants all lock their doors ...'

In a blur of motion Peter was up, leaping out of the window.

To his astonishment, he found himself back in the same room. 'What happened?' he asked, as Roberta once more aimed the saw at him.

'You cannot escape,' the ferret-faced man chuckled, 'for the simple reason that there is nowhere to escape to. Mmmf. You see, we are in a re-oriented universe, bounded by the walls of this room. *There is no outside.*'

The blonde moved closer, exuding an odor of musk. 'For that matter, darling, why try to escape?' she said. 'Wouldn't you rather stay here with me—always?'

'If this is a closed universe, what would we have to eat and drink?' asked Peter warily.

'We could live on love. Now put down your satchel and kiss me.'

'Nope. There's something phoney about you, woman. For one thing, your teeth look too real. And that musk. You seem to be exuding it through a single pore on your lovely alabaster neck.'

At that moment, Roberta's whole body began throwing off a deadly, high-voltage corona.

'A robot!' he exclaimed, leaping back. 'I should have known. Only robots call everybody darling.'

Her arms outstretched, she stumbled about the room after him. '... darling ...' she murmured. With all escape cut off, with her fire-crackling, million-volt arms reaching for him, Peter stumbled over a curiously-carved buddha, and the room disappeared!

He found himself seated under a blinding white light, while shadowy figures moved about him.

'Who are you? What are you doing here? What is in the—mmmf—the satchel?' asked the ferret's voice, full of scary echoes. Peter did not reply.

'A lovely girl you have. It would be a pity if anything happened to spoil her loveliness ...'

'You wouldn't dare!' Peter shouted, struggling to rise.

'Wouldn't I? What is your name?'

'Rumplestiltskin is my——' Something cracked him across the side of the head, a stunning blow that made bells ring and stars whirl.

The bells and stars were real. In the control room of the space ship, the alarm signalled a meteor swarm dead ahead.

Why isn't the ship automatically veering off? Peter wondered.

The answer was a shadowy figure hunched over the controls, keeping the steering wheel locked on course. It leered round at him, a ferine face with beady eyes and a cruel, mad smile.

'Unless you give me that satchel this instant I shall—mmmf—send us both to our deaths,' the little man chortled.

'Speaking of death,' said Peter, 'I have heard tales from the West Indies of animal zombies. For example, the Undead Duck.'

Deftly, Peter swung the satchel at the preoccupied face. The weasel was slapped to the floor, and the ship began to veer—but too late! Already the meteors were there, patiently boring into the hull!

At once, Peter shifted into reverse, minus the speed of light. Hurtling across the universe, his ship met its counterpart, moving at plus the speed of light. POW! Matter met anti-matter, and both exploded in a flash of light and anti-light! Zungg! Off went Peter at sidewise the speed of light, pursued by residual matter in the form of a slimy alien. It was all mush, with two beady antennae.

'Wait till I get my mandibles on you. Mmmf!' the alien thought at him.

'You've got another think coming,' Peter's mind shot back. 'I've been pursued by worse.'

'Really? Put down your satchel and tell me about it.'

Peter did not slacken his pace, but he began to spin his tale. He spoke of a time in India when he had been pursued by a giant, lumbering beast that was totally invisible—the Cello-phant!

But now the slimy alien was fast closing the gap between it and its prey! Seeing a lump of inert matter by the roadside, Peter dodged behind it and let the clumsy alien blunder on past.

'Whew!' he said, glancing at the lump of inert matter.

On closer inspection, it proved to be really a fast, late-model car. Peter leaped in and wheeled the machine down the road.

A speck appeared in the rear-view mirror, and grew to a taxi. 'It follows, that cab,' Peter said grimly. He speeded up, but the taxi continued to gain; now he could make out the driver's sharp nose and beady eyes. Peter knew he could never outrun the taxi, for it was no doubt a disguised ground-effect machine.

And dead ahead was Hairpin Turn. This spot had received its colorful name from the fact that one could throw a hairpin over its edge, and never hear it hit bottom. Often women came to toss bobbypins into the abyss, and listen in vain for their clatter. Just now, in fact, a lone woman stood at the brink, jettisoning *objets de coiffure* over the precipice, and unsuccessfully endeavoring to ascertain their collison with the ground. Disengaging a pin from her lovely auburn hair, she precipitated it into the chasm, and strained her ears without avail, to perceive its impact. She wore a trenchcoat.

As the taxi drew abreast of him, Peter cramped the wheel sharply, then braked to a halt. The taxi plunged into space and tumbled end over end, finally bursting into flames.

'Want a lift?' said Peter, eyeing the girl. Without a word she was in his arms, sobbing and pressing her burning lips to his.

As they drove away, he switched on the radio.

'—and partly cloudy. The most sensational news story of the day is the escape of condemned criminal Peter O'Hare, alias Jean Pierre Lapin, slated to die this noon by the guillotine. Police say the notorious satchel-thief made his escape this morning, from the midst of an interrogation. He is believed hiding out in parallel universes, other dimensions or the Paris sewers.'

The glove compartment popped open, and out stepped a small, stoat-like man holding an ugly automatic.

'Mmmf. Would you be so good as to hand over that satchel?' he said, his beady eyes regarding it hungrily. 'I shall reward you, of course—with death.'

'Have I told you about the Octicorn?' asked Peter. 'He is that strange beast of Idaho, having the body of a unicorn and the head of an octopus. He runs madly about, utterly harmless and annoying no one, waving his big flabby head about——'

'I do not care for animal jokes,' said the man coldly. 'Greta here and I are ingeniously-mutated, carefully trained foxes. Rather, I am a fox, and she is a vixen. I forget whether our children are called pups or cubs. While she stopped your car, I hid myself in your glove compartment. Sly, was it not?'

'A vixen!' Peter exclaimed. 'Why, the little minx!' He pinched Greta's cheek, and she bit his finger. 'Ow. This reminds me of an Arab I once knew, who ran a flea circus in Iran. Perhaps you've heard of the 1,001 Arabian Mites? No? Well, one day, one of them escaped. To make sure, the Arab had to count them. One mite, two mites, three mites ...'

Peter worked loose two wires from the dashboard. These he led back to the gas tank, while his story created the necessary diversion. Fishing a copper and a zinc penny from his pocket, he spit upon a piece of paper and placed it between them.

'Nine hundred ninety-eight mites, nine hundred ninety-nine mites ...' Pressing the two wires to his pennies, Peter flung himself from the car. He felt a blast of heat at his back, and a moment later, heard the distant roar, as the vehicle blew up.

'The old penny-battery trick always works,' he mused, watching a column of smoke rise from what once was Kansas City. Great clouds of locusts swept by him, on their way to devastate wheat fields and dominate the planet.

Peter rushed to his anti-grav machine, which opened to the image of his ear-print. As he lifted off, he felt he was not alone in the cabin. Keep calm, he thought, and continued to adjust the huge steam valves as if nothing were wrong. All the same he knew he was being watched by someone—or something. He turned.

And gasped. A Horrible Spore was rolling toward him, seeking food.

'Mmmf,' it roared.

There was no time for escape. Already the Spore's pseudopods were reaching for him. Peter's entire life passed before his eyes. Then, for the pseudopods had not yet clutched him, he speculated on the sort of life he could have had.

Roping steers. Reading billboards. Trading in my car, he thought, bitterly. Eating a hotdog, and throwing the wrapper into the Grand Canyon. Taking home movies of the wife and kids. For that matter, a wife and kids.

The Horrible Spore surrounded him, and began its peculiar pattern of digestion, a fission process. Peter was split into two duplicates of himself, and these fissioned in turn. Shortly there were inside the Spore a hundred thousand tiny hims.

Peter knew a bit of mob psychology. He knew that by nature they are quarrelsome and arrogant, willful and dissatisfied. Mobs long to plunder and burn; are terrible when frustrated, and in general, cowards. He keenly felt all these qualities within himselves.

There was nothing to plunder, and only the pseudostomach of the Spore to burn. Seizing torches, the crowd set fire to the Spore, which immediately disgorged them on a desert plain.

He had been pent up too long, and now he milled about, frustrated. Great droves of him threw down their satchels and wandered away, weeping, to die cowards' deaths. A few of him, however, took up the abandoned luggage and began piling it in great heaps. They began to quarrel over whether to plunder these satchels or burn them, and soon they were battling furiously.

It was difficult to tell friend from foe in the melée of fists and torches. Friend killed friend, and foe burned foe, until the sun went down on their madness. The last of them fell asleep by the embers of his late allies.

Her name-badge read 'Melissa Forbes'. She had long, ash-blonde hair and a lab coat that fitted well over soft breasts and hips. She was shaking him awake.

'Doctor, get up. We have work to do.'

'Hmm? Oh yes. Must have fallen asleep over the Fromminger equations. But who wouldn't?' He grinned, and Melissa caught her breath. Dr Peter O'Hare was well aware of the power of his crooked grin. 'Now where were we?'

'We must save the universe from certain destruction,' she said throatily, 'Two parallel universes have got off course.

They will collide in minutes, exploding into a drop of pure energy, unless——'

'Do you mean——?' he gasped, struggling into his own lab coat. One side had been cut away, to accommodate the satchel he always seemed to carry.

'Yes, Doctor. Only you can find a way out.'

A few calculations on his slide rule, and the scientist had done so. 'We will each go back into the past of one of the universes. There we will make the necessary adjustments to ensure that the two will never meet. Alas, we would never be able to return.'

'Then I can tell you,' she sobbed. 'Doctor, I love you.' A bright tear ran down her cheek and splashed into the test tube she grasped.

'Do you mean——?' he gasped, and took her in his arms.

'No.' She pushed him away. 'There isn't time, darling. If only you could give me some token of remembrance—say that satchel.'

Peter turned away to hide his own emotion, and as he did so, he realized the lab had only three walls! Where the fourth should have been was a dark void, filled with hostile, gleaming eyes. It was a trap, then. How well he knew the Lumpkinite police, with their combination lineup and psychodrama!

Snatching up a convenient gun, Peter fired into the crowd. 'Sic semper tyrannus!' he cried, leaping for the stage door.

'All well and good,' he said, pocketing the weapon, 'but how am I to get out of this hell?'

He realized for the first time that the incessant drumming had stopped. Those savages were surely up to some devilment, he thought.

A white man stepped out of a thicket. He wore a white, flowing robe and had a dissipated look about him.

'Are you by any chance the White God?' asked Peter.

'I am Virgil, come to guide you out of this hell.'

'Great Dante's ghost! What do they call this place, O noble Mantuan?'

The poet looked blank for a moment. 'Oh, the Slough of Despond, I guess. Here, Pilgrim, let me carry thy burden.'

'Hold this instead,' snarled Peter, and pumped eight slugs into Virgil. The poet assumed his true shape and scuttled away.

Adrian lay tied up in the alley behind the rocket terminal. As he loosened his bonds, Peter related the case to him.

'Rub your wrists to restore circulation, while I explain. They tied me up, too, and blindfolded me. They took me to another planet, but I counted the turns the space ship made, so I could find my way back. They're an unscrupulous gang of servo-mechanisms, all right. The old phonograph record was just a blind. What they really wanted was *the satchel itself.*'

'The satchel?'

'It's an antique, worth millions. The owner was stealing it from himself, to collect the insurance. But I wasn't sure, so I hid the old phonograph record.'

'Quick thinking, chief. Where did you hide it?'

'In the most obvious place—*Annie's old phonograph.*'

'Amazing! But how did you know he wasn't the real Virgil?' asked Adrian.

'He gave himself away when he mentioned the Slough of Despond. You see, William Faulkner didn't invent the name until years *after* the *real* John Bunyan's death. From there on, the rest was easy.'

Peter punched the dents out of Adrian's green hat and handed it to him. He held a pocket mirror while Adrian put on the hat. Then Peter reloaded his gun and put eight slugs in him.

Well, that's the spy game, he thought. The good die young. You never get rich, but you have your kicks. One week the Arcrusian space pirates get out of hand, and the next week, at about the same time, something rises out of the sea to nibble at Los Angeles.

I'll miss old Earth, though. Along about now it's turning into a ball of flame, as Lumpkin goes to war.

Chuckling, he pushed open the door of Annie's Earthside Bar.

1987 A.D.

'I don't know,' said James, lifting himself from the cushions scattered like bright leaves on the floor. 'I can't say that I'm really, you know, *happy*. Gin or something phoney?'

'Aw, man, don't give me decisions, give me drink,' said Porter. He lay across the black, tufted chaise that he called James's 'shrink couch'.

'Gin it is, then.' James thumbed a button, and a martini glass, frosty and edible-looking, slid into the wall niche and filled. Holding it by the stem, he passed it to Porter, then raised his shaggy brows at Marya.

'Nada,' she said. She was sprawled in a 'chair', really a piece of sculpture, and one of her bare feet had reached out to touch Porter's leg.

James made himself a martini and looked at it with distaste. If you broke this glass, he thought, it would not leave any sharp edges to, say, cut your wrists on.

'What was I saying? Oh—I can't say I'm really *happy*, but then I'm not—uh——'

'Sad?' volunteered Marya, peering from under the brim of her deerstalker.

'Depressed. I'm not depressed. So I must be happy,' he finished, and hid his confusion behind the glass. As he sipped, he looked her over, from her shapely calves to her ugly brown deerstalker. Last year at this time, she'd been wearing a baseball cap, blue with gold piping. It was easy to remember it, for this year all the girls in the Village were wearing baseball caps. Marya Katyovna was always ahead of the pack, in her dress as well as in her paintings.

'How do you know you're happy?' she said. 'Last week, I thought I was happy, too. I'd just finished my best work, and I tried to drown myself. The Machine pulled the drain. Then I was sad.'

'Why did you try to kill yourself?' James asked, trying to keep her in focus.

'I had this idea that after a perfect work, the artist should be destroyed. Dürer used to destroy the plates of his engravings, after a few impressions.'

'He did it for money,' muttered Porter.

'All right then, like that architect in Arabia. After he created his *magnum opus*, the Sultan had him blinded, so he couldn't do any cheap copies. See what I mean? An artist's life is supposed to lead toward his masterpiece, not away from it.'

Porter opened his eyes and said, 'Exist! The end of life is life. Exist, man, that's all you gotta do.'

'That sounds like cheap existentialism,' she snarled, withdrawing her foot. 'Porter, you are getting more and more like those damned Mussulmen.'

Porter smiled angrily and closed his eyes.

It was time to change the subject.

'Have you heard the one about the Martian who thought he was an earthman?' James said, using his pleasant-professional tone. 'Well, he went to his psychiatrist——'

As he went on with the joke, he studied the two of them. Marya was no worry, even with her dramatic suicide attempts. But Porter was a mess.

O. Henry Porter was his full adopted name, after some minor earlier writer. Porter was a writer, too, or had been. Up to a few months ago, he'd been considered a genius—one of the few of the twentieth century.

Something had happened. Perhaps it was the general decline in reading. Perhaps there was an element of self-defeat in him. For whatever reason, Porter had become little more than a vegetable. Even when he spoke, it was in the cheapest cliches of the old 'Hip' of twenty years ago. And he spoke less and less.

Vaguely, James tied it in with the Machines. Porter had been exposed to the therapeutic environment machines longer than most, and perhaps his genius was entangled with whatever they were curing. James had been too long away from his practice to guess how this was, but he recalled similar baby/bathwater cases.

'"So that's why it glows in the dark,"' James finished. As he'd expected, Marya laughed, but Porter only forced a smile, over and above his usual smirk of mystical bliss.

'It's an old joke,' James apologized.

'You are an old joke,' Porter enunciated. 'A headshrinker without no heads to shrink. What the hell do you do all day?'

'What's eating you?' said Marya to the ex-writer. 'What brought you up from the depths?'

James fetched another drink from the wall niche. Before bringing it to his lips, he said. 'I think I need some new friends.'

As soon as they were gone, he regretted his boorishness. Yet somehow there seemed to be no reason for acting human any more. He was no longer a psychiatrist, and they were not his patients. Any little trauma he might have wreaked would be quickly repaired by their Machines. Even so, he'd have made an extra effort to sidestep the neuroses of his friends if he were not able to dial FRIENDS and get a new set.

Only a few years had passed since the Machines began seeing to the happiness, health and continuation of the human race, but he could barely remember life before Them. In the dusty mirror of his unused memory, there remained but a few clear spots. He recalled his work as a psychiatrist on the Therapeutic Environment tests.

He recalled the argument with Brody.

'Sure, they work on a few test cases. But so far these gadgets haven't done anything a qualified psychiatrist couldn't do,' said James.

'Agreed,' said his superior. 'but they haven't made any mistakes, either. Doctor, these people are cured. Morever, they're happy!'

Frank envy was written all over Bro Brody's heavy face. James knew his superior was having trouble with his wife again.

'But, Doctor,' James began, 'these people are *not* being taught to deal with their environment. Their environment is learning to deal with them. That isn't medicine, it's spoon-feeding!

'When someone is depressed, he gets a dose of Ritalin, bouncy tunes on the Muzik, and some dear friend drops in on him unexpectedly. If he is manic or violent, he gets Thorazine, sweet music, melancholy stories on TV, and maybe a cool bath. If he's bored, he gets excitement; if he's frustrated, he gets something to break; if——'

Brody interrupted. 'All right,' he said. 'Let me ask you the sixty-four-dollar question: Could you do better?'

No one could do better. The vast complex of Therapeutic Environment Machines which grew up advanced Medicine a millenium in a year. The government took control, to ensure that anyone of however modest means could have at his disposal the top specialists in the country, with all the latest data and techniques. In effect, these specialists were on duty round-the-clock in each patient's home, keeping him alive, healthy, and reasonably happy.

Nor were they limited to treatment. The Machines had extensions clawing through the jungles of the world, spying on witch-doctors and learning new medicines. Drug and dietary research became their domain, as did scientific farming and birth control. By 1985, when it became manifest that machines could and did run everything better, and that nearly everyone in the country wanted to be a patient, the U.S. government capitulated. Other nations followed suit.

By now, no one worked at all, so far as James knew. They had one and only one duty—to be happy.

And happy they were. One's happiness was guaranteed, by every relay and transistor from those that ran one's air-conditioner right up to those in the chief complex of computers called MEDCENTRAL in Washington—or was it the Hague, now? James had not read a newspaper since people had stopped killing each other, since the news had dwindled to weather and sports. In fact, he'd stopped reading the newspaper when the M.D. Employment Wanted ads began to appear.

There were no jobs, only Happiness Jobs—make-work invented by the Machines. In such a job, one could never find an insoluble, or even difficult problem. One finished one's daily quota without tiring one's mind or body. Work was no longer work, it was therapy, and, as such, it was constantly rewarding.

Happiness, normality. James saw the personalities of all people drifting downward, like so many different snowflakes falling at last into the common, shapeless mound.

'I'm drunk, that's all,' he said aloud. 'Alcohol's a depressant. Need another drink.'

He lurched slightly as he crossed the room to the niche. The floor must have detected it, for instead of a martini, his pressing the button drew blood from his thumb. In a second, the wall had analyzed his blood and presented him with a glass of liquid. A sign lit: 'Drink this down at once. Replace glass on sink.'

He drained the pleasant-tasting liquid and at once felt drowsy and warm. Somehow he found his way to the bedroom, the door moving to accomodate him, and he fell into bed.

As soon as James R. Fairchild, AAAAGTR-RHOLA was asleep, mechanisms went into action to save his life. That is, he was in no immediate danger, but MED 8 reported his decrease in life expectancy by ·00005 years as a result of over-indulgence, and MED 19 evaluated his behaviour, recorded on magnetic tape, as increasing his suicide index by a dangerous 15 points. A diagnostic unit detached itself from the bathroom wall and carreened into the bedroom, halting silently and precisely by his side. It drew more blood, checked pulse, temp, resp, heart and brain-wave pattern, and x-rayed his abdomen. Not instructed to go on to patcolar reflexes, it packed up and zoomed away.

In the living-room, a housekeeper buzzed about its work, destroying the orange cushions, the sculpture, the couch and the carpet. The walls took on an almost imperceptibly warmer tone. The new carpet matched them.

The furniture—chosen and delivered without the sleeping man's knowledge—was Queen Anne, enough to crowd the room. Its polyethlene wraps were left on while the room was disinfected.

In the kitchen, PHARMO 9 ordered and received a new supply of anti-depressants.

It was always the sound of a tractor that awoke Lloyd Young, and though he knew it was an artificial sound, it cheered him all the same. Almost made his day start right. He lay and listened to it awhile before opening his eyes.

Hell, the real tractors didn't make no sound at all. They worked in the night, burrowing along and plowing a field in one hour that would take a man twelve. Machines pumped strange new chemicals into the soil, and applied heat, to force two full crops of corn in one short Minnesota summer.

There wasn't much use being a farmer, but he'd always wanted to have a farm, and the Machines said you could have what you wanted. Lloyd was about the only man in these parts still living in the country by now, just him and twelve cows and a half-blind dog, Joe. There wasn't much to do, with Them running it all. He could go watch his cows being milked, or walk down with Joe to fetch the mail, or watch TV. But it was quiet and peaceful, the way he liked it.

Except for Them and Their pesky ways. They'd wanted to give Joe a new set of machine eyes, but Lloyd said no, if the good Lord wanted him to see, he'd never have blinded him. That was just the way he'd answered Them about the heart operation, too. Seemed almost like They didn't have enough to keep 'em busy, or something. They was always worrying about him, him who took real good care of himself all through M.I.T. and twenty years of engineering.

When They'd automated, he'd been done out of a job, but he couldn't hold that against Them. If Machines was better engineers than him, well, shoot——!

He opened his eyes and saw he'd be late for milking if he

didn't look sharp. Without even thinking, he chose the baby blue overalls with pink piping from his wardrobe, jammed a blue straw hat on his head, and loped out to the kitchen.

His pail was by the door. It was a silver one today—yesterday it had been gold. He decided he liked the silver better, for it made the milk look cool and white.

The kitchen door wouldn't budge, and Lloyd realized it meant for him to put on his shoes. Damnit, he'd of liked to go barefoot. Damnit, he would of.

He would of liked to do his own milking, too, but They had explained how dangerous it was. Why, you could get kicked in the head before you knew it! Reluctantly, the Machines allowed him to milk, each morning, one cow that had been tranquilized and all its legs fastened in a steel frame.

He slipped on his comfortable blue brogans and picked up his pail again. This time the kitchen door opened easily, and as it did, a rooster crowed in the distance.

Yes, there had been a lot of doors closed in Lloyd's face. Enough to have made a bitter man of him, but for Them. He knew They could be trusted, even if they had done him out of his job in nineteen and seventy. For ten years, he had just bummed around, trying to get factory work, anything. At the end of his rope, until they saved him.

In the barn, Betsy, his favorite Jersey, had been knocked out and shackled by the time he arrived. The Muzik played a bouncy, lighthearted tune, perfect for milking.

No, it wasn't Machines that did you dirt, he knew. It was people. People and animals, live things always trying to kick you in the head. As much as he liked Joe and Betsy, which was more than he liked people, he didn't really trust 'em.

You could trust Machines. They took good care of you. The only trouble with Them was—well, they *knew* so much. They were always so damned smart and busy, They made you feel kind of useless. Almost like you were standing in their light.

It was altogether an enjoyable ten minutes, and when he stepped into the cool milkhouse to empty the pail into a receptacle that led God knew where, Lloyd had a strange impulse. He wanted to taste the warm milk, something he'd promised not to do. They had warned him about diseases, but he just felt too good to worry this morning. He tilted the silver pail to his lips——

And a bolt of lightning knocked it away, slamming him to the floor. At least it felt like a bolt of lightning. He tried to get up and found he couldn't move. A green mist began spraying from the ceiling. Now what the hell was that? he wondered, and drifted off to sleep in the puddle of spilled milk.

The first MED unit reported no superficial injuries. Lloyd C. Young, AAAAMTL-RH01AB was resting well, pulse high, resp normal. MED 8 disinfected the area thoroughly and destroyed all traces of the raw milk. While MED 19 pumped his stomach and swabbed nose, throat, oesophagus and trachea, MED 8 cut away and destroyed all his clothing. An emergency heating unit warmed him until fresh clothing could be constructed. Despite the cushioned floor, the patient had broken a toe in falling. It was decided not to move him, but to erect bed and traction on the spot. MED 19 recommended therapeutic punishment.

When Lloyd awoke, the television came to life, showing an amiable-looking man with white hair.

'You have my sympathy,' the man said. 'You have just survived what we call a "Number-One Killer Accident", a bad fall in your home. Our machines were in part responsible for this, in the course of saving your life from——' The man hesitated, while a sign flashed behind him: 'BACTERIAL POISONING.' Then he went on, '—by physically removing you from the danger. Since this was the only course open to us, your injury could not have been avoided.

'*Except by you*. Only *you* can save your life, finally.' The man pointed at Lloyd. 'Only *you* can make all of modern science worthwhile. And only *you* can help lower our shocking death toll. You will cooperate, won't you? Thank you.' The screen went dark, and the set dispensed a pamphlet.

It was a complete account of his accident, and a warning

about unpasteurized milk. He would be in bed for a week, it said, and urged him to make use of his telephone and FRIENDS.

Professor David Wattleigh sat in the tepid water of his swimming pool in Southern California and longed to swim. But it was forbidden. The gadgets had some way of knowing what he was doing, he supposed, for every time he immersed himself deeper than his chest, the motor of the resuscitator clattered a warning from poolside. It sounded like the snarl of a sheep-dog. Or perhaps, he reflected, a Hound of Heaven, an anti-Mephistopheles, come to tempt him into virtue.

Wattleigh sat perfectly still for a moment, then reluctantly he heaved his plump pink body out of the water. Ah, it was no better than a bath. As he passed into the house, he cast a glance of contempt and loathing at the squat machine.

It seemed as if anything he wished to do were forbidden. Since the day he'd been forced to abandon Nineteenth-Century English Literature, the constraints of *mechanica* had tightened about Wattleigh, closing him off from his old pleasures one by one. Gone were his pipe and port, his lavish luncheons, his morning swim. In place of his library, there now existed a kind of vending machine that each day 'vended' him two pages of thoroughly bowdlerized Dickens. Gay, colorful, witty passages they were, too, set in large Schoolbook type. They depressed him thoroughly.

Yet he had not given up entirely. He pronounced anathema upon the Machines in every letter he wrote to Delphinia, an imaginary lady of his acquaintance, and he feuded with the dining-room about his luncheons.

If the dining-room did not actually withhold food from him, it did its best to take away his appetite. At various times, it had painted itself bilious yellow, played loud and raucous music and flashed portraits of naked fat people upon its walls. Each day it had some new trick to play, and each day, Wattleigh outwitted it.

Now he girded on his academic gown and entered the dining-room, prepared for battle. Today, he saw, the room was upholstered in green velvet and lit by a gold chandelier. The dining table was heavy, solid oak, unfinished. There was not a particle of food upon it.

Instead there was a blonde, comely woman.

'Hello,' she said, jumping down from the table. 'Are you Professor David Wattleigh? I'm Helena Hershee, from New York. I got your name through FRIENDS, and I just had to look you up.'

'I—how do you do?' he stammered. By way of answer, she unzipped her dress.

MED 19 approved what followed as tending to weaken that harmful delusion, 'Delphinia'. MED 8 projected a year of treatment, and found the resultant weight loss could add as much as 12 years to patient Wattleigh's life.

After Helena had gone to sleep, the Professor played a few games with the Ideal Chessplayer. Wattleigh had once belonged to a chess club, and he did not want to lose touch with the game entirely. And one did get rusty. He was amazed at how many times the Ideal Chessplayer had to actually cheat to let him win.

But win he did, game after game, and the Ideal Chessplayer each time would wag its plastic head from side to side and chuckle, 'Well, you really got me that time, Wattleigh. Care for another?'

'No,' said Wattleigh, finally disgusted. Obediently the machine folded its board into its chest and rolled off somewhere.

Wattleigh sat at his desk and started a letter to Delphinia.

'My Darling Delphinia,' scratched his old steel pen on the fine, laid paper. 'Today a thought occurred to me while I was bathing at Brighton. I have often told you, and as often complained of the behaviour of my servant, M——. It, for I cannot bring myself to call it "him" or "she", has been most distressing about my writing to you, even to the point of blunting my pens and hiding my paper. I have not discharged it for this disgraceful show, for I am bound to it—yes, *bound* to it by a strange and terrible secret fate that makes me doubt at times which is master and which, man. It reminds one of several old comedies, in which, man and master having changed roles, and maid and mistress likewise, they meet. I mean, of course, in the works of——'

Here the letter proper ended, for the professor could think of no name to fit. After writing, and lining out, 'Dickens, Dryden, Dostoyevsky, Racine, Rousseau, Camus,' and a dozen more, his inkwell ran dry. He knew it would be no use to inquire after more ink, for the Machine was dead set against this letter——

Looking out the window, he saw a bright pink-and-yellow striped ambulance. So, the doctor next door was going off to zombie-land, was he? Or, correctly, to the Hospital for the Asocial. In the East, they called them 'Mussulmen'; here, 'zombies', but it all came to the same thing: the living dead, who needed no elaborate houses, games, ink. They needed only intravenous nourishment, and little of that. The drapes drew themselves, so Wattleigh knew the doctor was being carried out then. He finished his interrupted thought.

—and in any case, he was wholly dissatisfied with this letter. He had not mentioned Helena, luncheon, his resuscitator which growled at him, and so much more. Volumes more, if only he had the ink to write, if only his memory would not fail him when he sat down to write, if only——

James stood with his elbow on the marble mantlepiece of Marya's apartment, surveying the other guests and sizing them up. There was a farmer from Minnesota, incredibly dull, who claimed to have once been an engineer, but who hardly knew what a slide rule was. There was Marya in the company of some muscular young man James disliked at sight, an ex-mathematician named Dewes or Clewes. Marya was about to play chess with a slightly plump Californian, while his girl, a pretty little blonde thing called Helena Hershee, stood by to kibitz.

'I'm practically a champion,' explained Wattleigh, setting up the pieces. 'So perhaps I ought to give you a rook or two.'

'If you like,' said Marya. 'I haven't played in years. About all I remember is the Fool's Mate.'

James drifted over to Helena's side and watched the game.

'I'm James Fairchild,' he said, and added almost defiantly, 'M.D.'

Helena's lips, too bright with lipstick, parted. 'I've heard of you,' she murmured. 'You're the aggressive Dr Fairchild who runs through friends so fast, aren't you?'

Marya's eyes came up from the game. Seemingly her eyes had no pupils, and James guessed she was full of Ritalin. 'James is not in the least aggressive,' she said. 'But he gets mad when you won't let him psychoanalyze you.'

'Don't disturb the game,' said Wattleigh. He put both elbows on the table in an attitude of concentration.

Helena had not heard Marya's remark. She had turned to watch the muscular mathematician lecture Lloyd.

'Hell yes. The Machines got to do all the bearing and raising of children. Otherwise, we'd have a population explosion, you get me? I mean, we'd run out of food——'

'You really pick 'em, Marya,' said James. He gestured at the young man. 'Whatever became of that "writer"? Porter, was it? Christ, I can still hear him saying, "exist, man!"' James snorted.

Marya's head came up once more, and tears stood in her pupilless eyes. 'Porter went to the hospital. He's a Mussulman, now,' she said brightly. 'I wish I could feel something for him, but They won't let me.'

'—it's like Malthus's law, or somebody's law. Animals grow faster than vegetables,' the mathematician went on, speaking to the farmer.

'Checkmate,' said Marya, and bounced to her feet. 'James, have you a Sugarsmoke? Chocolate?'

He produced a bright orange cigar. 'Only Bitter Orange, I'm afraid. Ask the Machine.'

'I'm afraid to ask it for anything, today,' she said. 'It keeps drugging me—James, Porter was put away a month ago, and I haven't been able to paint since. Do you think I'm crazy? The Machine thinks so.'

'The Machine,' he said, tearing off the end of the cigar with his teeth, 'is always right.'

Seeing Helena had wandered away to sit on Marya's Chinese sofa, he excused himself with a nod and followed.

Wattleigh still sat brooding over the Fool's Mate. 'I don't understand. I just can't understand,' he said.

'—it's like the Hare and the Tortoise,' boomed the mathematician. Lloyd nodded solemnly. 'The slow one can't ever catch up, see?'

Lloyd spoke. 'Well, you got a point. You got a point. Only I thought the slow one was the winner.'

'Oh.' Dewes (or Clewes) lapsed into thoughtful silence.

Marya wandered about the room, touching faces as if she were a blind person looking for someone she knew.

'But I don't understand!' said Wattleigh.

'I do,' James mumbled about the cigar. The bittersweet smoke was thick as liquid in his mouth. He understood, all right. He looked at them, one by one: An ex-mathematician having trouble with the difference between arithmetic and geometry; an ex-engineer, ditto; a painter not allowed to paint, not even to feel; a former chess 'champion' who could not play. And that left Helena Hershee, mistress to poor, dumb Wattleigh.

'Before the Machines——?' he began.

'—I was a judge,' she said, running her fingertips over the back of his neck provocatively. 'And you? What kind of doctor were you?'

1988 A.D.

'It was during the second world war,' Jim Fairchild said. He lay on his back on the long, tiger-striped sofa, with a copy of HOT ROD KOMIKS over his eyes.

'I thought it only started in the sixties,' said Marya.

'Yeah, but the *name*, "Mussulman"—that started in the Nazi death camps. There were some people in them who couldn't—you know—get with it. They stopped eating and seeing and hearing. Everybody called them "Mussulmen", because they seemed like Moslems, mystic . . .'

His voice trailed off, for he was thinking of the second world war. The good old days, when a man made his own rules. No Machines to tell you what to do.

He had been living with Marya for several months, now. She was his girl, just as the other Marya, in HOT ROD KOMIKS, was the girl of the other Jim, Jim (Hell-On-Wheels) White. It was a funny thing about Komiks. They were real life, and at the same time, they were better than life.

Marya—his Marya—was no intellectual. She didn't like to read and think, like Jim, but that was o.k., because men were supposed to do all the reading and thinking and fighting and killing. Marya sat in a lavender bucket seat in the corner, drawing with her crayons. Easing his lanky, lean body up off the sofa, Jim walked around behind her and looked at the sketch.

'Her nose is crooked,' he said.

'That doesn't matter, silly. This is a fashion design. It's only the dress that counts.'

'Well, how come she's got yellow hair? People don't have yellow hair.'

'Helena Hershee has.'

'No she hasn't!'

'She has so?'

'No, it ain't yellow, it's—it ain't yellow.'

Then they both paused, because Muzik was playing their favorite song. Each had a favorite of his own—Jim's was 'Blap', and Marya's was 'Yes I Know I Rilly Care For You'—but they had one favorite together. Called 'Kustomized Tragedy'. It was one of the songs in which the Muzik imitated their voices, singing close harmony:

Jim Gunn had a neat little kustom job,
And Marya was his girl.
They loved each other with a love so true
The truest in the worl'.
But Jim weren't allowed to drive his kar,
And Marya could not see;
Kust'mized Traju-dee-ee-ee.

The song went on to articulate how Jim Gunn wanted more than anything in the worl' to buy an eye operation for his girl, who wished to admire his kustom kar. So he drove to a store and held it up, but someone recognized his kar. The police shot him, but:

He kissed his Marya one last time;
The policeman shot her, too.
But she said, 'I can see your kustom, Jim!
It's pretty gold and bloo!'
He smiled and died embracing her,
Happy that she could see.
Kust'mized Traju-dee.

Of course, in real life, Marya could see very well, Jim had no kar, and there were no policemen. But it was true for them, nevertheless. In some sense they could not express, they felt their love was a tragedy.

Knowing Jim felt lonesome and bloo, Marya walked over and kissed his ear. She lay down beside him, and at once they were asleep.

MEDCENTRAL's audit showed a population of 250 million in NORTHAMER, stabilized. Other than a few incubator failures, and one vatt of accidentally-infected embryos, progress was as predicted, with birth and death rates equal. The norm had shifted once more toward the asocial, and UTERINE CONTROL showed 90·2% adult admission at both major hospitals.

Trenchant abnormals were being regressed through adolescence, there being no other completely satisfactory method of normalizing them without shock therapy, with its attendant contraindications.

Lloyd pulled his pocket watch from the bib of his plaid overalls. The hands of Chicken Licken pointed straight up, meaning there was just time to fetch the mail before Farm

Kartoons on TV. On impulse, Lloyd popped the watch into his mouth and chewed. It was delicious, but it gave him little pleasure. Everything was too easy, too soft. He wanted exciting things to happen to him, like the time on Farm Kartoons when Black Angus tried to kill the hero, Lloyd White by breaking up his Machine, and Lloyd White had stabbed him with a pitchfork syringe and sent him off to the hospital.

Mechanical Joe, knowing it was time to fetch the mail, came running out of the house. He wagged his tail and whined impatiently. It didn't make any difference that he wasn't a real dog, Lloyd thought as they strolled toward the mailbox. Joe still liked it when you scratched his ears. You could tell, just by the look in his eyes. He was livelier and a lot more fun than the first Joe.

Lloyd paused a moment, remembering how sad he'd been when Joe died. It was a pleasantly melancholy thought, but now mechanical Joe was dancing around him and barking anxiously. They continued.

The mailbox was chock-full of mail. There was a new komik, called LLOYD FARMER AND JOE, and a whole big box of new toys.

Yet later, when Lloyd had read the komik and watched Farm Kartoon and played awhile with his building set, he still felt somehow heavy, depressed. It was no good being alone all the time, he decided. Maybe he should go to New York and see Jim and Marya. Maybe the Machines there were different, not so bossy.

For the first time, another, stranger thought came to him. Maybe he should go *live* in New York.

'DEAR DELPHINIA,' Dave printed. 'THIS IS GOING TO BE MY LAST LETTER TO YOU, AS I DONT LOVE YOU ANY MORE. *I* KNOW NOW WHAT HAS BEEN MAKING ME FEEL BAD, AND IT IS YOU. YOU ARE REALLY MY MASHINE, ARENT YOU HA HA I'LL BET YOU DIDNT THINK I NEW.

'NOW I LOVE HELENA MORE THAN YOU AND WE ARE GOING AWAY TO NEW YORK AND SEE LOTS OF FRIENDS AND GO TO

LOTS OF PARTYS AND HAVE LOTS OF FUN AND I DONT CARE IF I DONT SEE YOU NO MORE.

'LOVE, AND BEST OF LUCK TO A SWELL KID,

'DAVE W.'

After an earthquake destroyed 17 million occupants of the western hospital, MEDCENTRAL ordered the rest moved at once to the east. All abnormals not living near the east hospital were also persuaded to evacuate to New York. Persuasion was as follows:

Gradually, humidity and pressure were increased to ·9 discomfort, while subliminally, pictures of New York were flashed on all surfaces around each patient.

Dave and Helena had come by subway from L.A., and they were tired and cross. The subway trip itself took only two or three hours, but they had spent an additional hour in the taxi to Jim and Marya's.

'It's an electric taxi,' Dave explained,' and it only goes about a mile an hour. I'll sure never make that trip again.'

'I'm glad you came,' said Marya. 'We've been feeling terrible lonesome and bloo.'

'Yes,' Jim added,' and I got an idea. We can form a club, see, against the Machines. I got it all figured out. We——'

'Babay, tell them about the zombies—I mean, the Mussulmen,' said Helena.

Dave spoke with an excited, wild look about him. 'Jeez, yeah, they had about a million cars of them on the train, all packed in glass bottles. I wasn't sure what the hell they were at first, see, so I went up and looked at one. It was a skinny, hairless man, all folded up in a bottle inside another bottle. Weird-looking.'

In honor of their arrival, the Muzik played the favorite songs of all four: 'Zonk', 'Yes I Know I Rilly Care For You', 'Blap' and 'That's My Babay', while the walls went transparent for a moment, showing a breathtaking view of the gold towers of New York. Lloyd, who spoke to no one, sat in the corner keeping time to the music. He had no favorite song.

'I want to call this the Jim Fairchild Club,' said Jim. 'The purpose of this here club is to get rid of the Machines. Kick 'em out!'

Marya and Dave sat down to a game of chess.

'I know how we can do it, too,' Jim went on. 'Here's my plan: Who put the Machines in, in the first place? The U.S. Government. Well, there ain't any U.S. government any more. So the Machines are illegal. Right?'

'Right,' said Helena. Lloyd continued to tap his foot, though no Muzik was playing.

'They're outlaws,' said Jim. 'We oughta kill them!'

'But how?' asked Helena.

'I ain't got all the details worked out yet. Give me time. Because you know, the Machines done us wrong.'

'How's that?' asked Lloyd, as if from far away.

'We all had good jobs, and we were smart. A long time ago. Now we're all getting dumb. You know?'

'That's right,' Helena agreed. She opened a tiny bottle and began painting her toenails.

'I think,' said Jim, glaring about him, 'the Machines are trying to make us all into Mussulmen. Any of you want to get stuffed into a bottle? Huh?'

'A bottle inside a bottle,' Dave corrected, without looking up from his game.

Jim continued, 'I think the Machines are drugging us into Mussulmen. Or else they got some kind of ray, maybe, that makes us stupider. An x-ray, maybe.'

'We gotta do something,' said Helena, admiring her foot.

Marya and Dave began to quarrel about how the pawn moves.

Lloyd continued to tap his foot, marking time.

1989 A.D.

Jimmy had a good idea, but nobody wanted to listen. He remembered once when he was an itsy boy, a egg machine that tooked the eggs out of their shells and putted them into plastic —things. It was funny, the way the machine did that. Jimmy didn't know why it was so funny, but he laughed and laughed, just thinking about it. Silly, silly, silly eggs.

Marya had a idea, a real good one. Only she didn't know how to say it so she got a crayon and drew a great Big! picture of the Machines: Mommy Machine and Daddy Machine and all the little Tiny Tot Machines.

Loy-Loy was talking. He was building a block house. 'Now I'm putting the door,' he said. 'Now I'm putting the lit-tle window. Now the—why is the window littler than the house? I don't know. This is the chimney and this is the stee-ple and open the door and where's all the peo-ple? I don't know.'

Helena had a wooden hammer, and she was driving all the pegs. Bang! Bang! Bang! 'One, two, three!' she said. 'Banga-banga-bang!'

Davie had the chessmen out, lined up in rows, two by two. He wanted to line them all up three by three, only somehow he couldn't. It made him mad and he began to cry.

Then one of the Machines came and stuck something in his mouth, and everybody else wanted one and somebody was screaming and more Machines came and...

The coded message came to MEDCENTRAL. The last five abnormals had been cured, and all physical and mental functions reduced to the norm. All pertinent data on them were switched over to UTERINE SUPPLY, which clocked them in at 400 hours G.M.T., day 1, year 1989. MEDCENTRAL agreed on the time-check, then switched itself off.

As Edward Sankey stepped from his limousine, he involuntarily glanced up. The sky was a flat, glazed blue, empty of clouds. The corner of his eye caught movement: a ragged line of specks. Birds? He did not wish to look directly at them to find out. Lowering the black brim of his homburg against them, Sankey moved on into the courthouse.

Preston, the other committee member, was already at his table, laying out batches of documents like a game of solitaire. These would be new depositions from witnesses of the alleged migrations. Preston seemed to be sorting them by some intricate system of his own.

'You look as if you had a rough night, Ed,' he murmured. 'Hope you're ready to hear our last witnesses today. I think we can wrap up the report by Thursday afternoon and get a long weekend out of this.'

'I—something happened last night, Harry.' Sankey dropped into a chair and unfastened the top button of his overcoat with gloved fingers. 'I—I think I saw something myself. And not only that, I——'

'Haven't got time to go into it now, old sport. We've got fifty witnesses out there to interview, and all these statements to read. Try to pull yourself together for now, and you can tell me all about it at lunch.'

Sankey tried to take his partner's advice. Yet all through the morning, even as he listened to testimony, he found his thoughts filled with the events of last night.

He was sitting in the reading nook, a warmer, cozier room than his library. At midnight Sankey found himself dozing over a lukewarm cup of chocolate and the report, in execrable police English, of one Patrolman H. L. Weems:

'We received a call from the protection agency who handles

the Waxman Collection of manuscripts. They reported a broken window. We proceeded to the scene. We arrived at 10.45. No other doors or windows were open. The broken glass lay outside, like the window was broken outwards. There was a book found lying in the grass. Subsequently we found no other book missing. The book was damaged by broken glass. It was a copy of *The Nürnburg Chronicle*, a rare book and one of the first printed books.'

Suddenly Edward caught his breath. The sound—if a sound there had been—seemed to come from the library. Marian, he supposed, looking for a sleep-inducing novel.

The final witnesses were government experts. Bates of the Wildlife Commission was a small, balding man with clownish tufts of hair over his ears and circumflex eyebrows that made him seem utterly astonished by everything he saw.

'As this chart shows, the migrations are not just southward, but toward a specific point in the Brazilian jungle. The density of migrants increases proportionately as one approaches this point. We have asked the Air Force to overfly this area and report, but it seems conventional planes were unable to get through. The air is literally filled with—ah—migrants.'

'What about high-altitude reconnaissance planes?' Preston asked, his voice hoarse from the week's strain.

'They have flown over and photographed the area extensively, but the photographs show nothing of special import.'

The thumping began again. Sankey frowned, looking at a report of dubious significance:

'Librarian Emma Thwart, 51, reports an unknown assailant hurled a large dictionary at her from behind. The accompanying photos are of Miss Thwart's shoulder bruises. If . . .'

There was a crash of glass, and Sankey came to his feet. Moving almost automatically to the closet, he selected a golf club and crept to the library door. He turned out the light behind him, slipped an arm inside the door and switched on the library light. In one movement, he kicked the door back and ducked.

There was no one in the room. One pane high in the French windows had been broken, but they appeared to be still locked. Four or five bound volumes of early quarterlies were missing from one end of the shelf, he noticed, including the first volumes of *Dial* and *Transition*. They would be costly to replace, he thought, glancing around.

Something struck him in the back of the head, hard. He fell, recalling for no reason the photos of Miss Thwart's bruises. . . .

Mr Tone of the Library of Congress was speaking.

'We seem to have a correlation between the migrants and the rate of book usage—a negative correlation, I might add,' he said in a pompous voice. 'We thus find that the rare book collections are hardest hit. It is no surprise to learn that the "remaindered" shelves of bookstores are being picked clean.' He handed out Mimeographed sheets of statistics.

'But isn't it a fact, Mr Tone, that the rate of migrations has actually increased? And wouldn't this imply that more books of all types are disappearing?'

Tone licked papery lips with a pale tongue. 'Yes. And in fact, the books now disappearing are progressively more well-used types. According to our latest estimates, the entire book output of the world will be gone by'—he checked a notebook—'by the twenty-second of this month.'

'That's Friday, isn't it?' asked Preston.

'Yes, I believe so.'

'Right. We'll put it into the record as Friday, the twenty-second of April.'

Sankey felt he had not been unconscious for more than a few seconds, yet the entire shelf of quarterlies was now missing. He staggered to his feet, the useless mashie still gripped in his fist, and looked about for his assailant.

There was a noise down behind the desk, as of a bird beating its broken wing against the floor. He yanked the desk back and raised the iron.

Volume I of Gibbon's *The Decline and Fall of the Roman Empire* flopped back and forth, fanning its leaves madly. The binding was broken and torn—no doubt from smashing his window or knocking him down! So this was what had helped the quarterlies escape! Sankey tried to think of his blood pressure, but suddenly all his thought was concentrated in the fingers that held the golf club. Savagely he whipped it down at the fluttering thing on the floor, again and again, watching its thrashing cover pulp and shred...

The witnesses, amateur and expert, had strong views on the causes of the migrations. While many of the amateurs gave supernatural explanations or referred to rats leaving a sinking ship, the *deformation professional* was clearly no less responsible for many distorted opinions. A psychologist insisted that cold war hysteria and the stress of modern living were producing mass hallucinations; people were unknowingly destroying or hiding books, he said.

A meteorologist tried to relate the migrations to atmospheric disturbances caused by sunspot activity. Even when his 'peculiar wind' theory was proven inadequate, he clung to it childishly.

Bates of the Wildlife Commission hazarded a guess that the books were trying to return to a state of nature. 'It makes sense,' he insisted. 'They came from trees. Who knows but what they've been conscious, if only on some chemical level, of their origins? They've been longing to return to the jungle, and now they are doing it.'

Mr Tone wondered if books felt unloved and rejected.

'These educational materials,' he said. 'They stand there, week after week, unread. How would you feel? You'd commit suicide. And that is just what they are doing, killing themselves like lemmings. I've been around books all my life, and I think I'm qualified to say I understand them.'

Sedley of the N.A.S.A. explained how books flew, but was reluctant to assign a meaning to their flight. 'The way we figure it, they convert some small part of their mass into energy, in some way we don't understand yet. Then they just —well, just flap their covers.

'Anything flat can fly, that part is easy. But as for *why* they fly, I'd hate to guess. Maybe Russia could answer that question quicker than I can. I say no more.'

Marian was watching the migrations on television when Sankey reached home that evening.

'Telephone books over Florida,' she said gaily. 'Millions of them, darling.'

He glanced at the large, slow-flapping, graceful creatures for only a moment before going directly up to bed. Later he would get up to try dealing with the final batch of reports, he promised himself.

The ache in the back of his head was worse when he awoke late in the evening. Though Sankey tried to examine reports in the reading nook, his vision was blurred with pain, and he could not ignore the thumping sounds from the library.

Marian looked in to say good-night.

'If you want a book, dear,' he said carefully, 'you'd better let me get it for you. The library really isn't safe tonight.'

'Oh, goodness no!' she said. 'I wouldn't think of letting you go in there again for any reason! Anyway, I'm getting to sleep early tonight, I hope. Big doings in town tomorrow.'

'Eh? What's that?'

'They say there's a really huge flock passing over the city at noon.'

Sankey and Preston worked on the draft of their report for only two hours. At 11.30 they were out on the courthouse roof with binoculars. A dark cloud front along the horizon was, Preston claimed, the forefront of the flock. Sankey trained his binoculars downward, on the crowds.

'There certainly is a holiday atmosphere down there,' he observed. 'It's as if they were waiting for a parade.' He realized even as he said it that he, too, felt that way. Unaccountably, the air had a savor of expected joy for him. He examined his bubbly feelings and questioned them. How ridiculous! What did he come out to see? He ought to go inside and work—but he kept his seat on the parapet.

Below him, traffic was stalled for miles in every direction, and pedestrians had spilled out into the street. Many drivers had given up, switched off their engines and climbed upon their car roofs to watch. Here and there were people with books under their arms; they would probably release them to see if they joined the flock. Hawkers moved up and down, dispensing cheap paperbacks from cartons.

'Here they come!' Harry Preston cried, leaping up. The cloud had advanced, and now Sankey could see the individual particles of which it was made. Through binoculars he could just make out the shapes of the leaders, which were now flapping steadily. They rose in an heroic effort to pull the flock up enough to clear the city. These were strong, heavy, cloth-bound ledgers and reference works, and the books rising behind them, he guessed by their wedge formations, would be encyclopedias. There were perhaps ten thousand sets, perhaps a million, he could not guess. A court-house window smashed somewhere below; a set of law references rose in a lazy spiral, beating their strong, hard covers.

Myriads of volumes of all types came on then, grouped now by color, now by age. He noted one giant hymnal, its parchment leaves opening downward to expose square, black single notes, each larger than a human hand. It was accompanied by a host of tiny old psalters or books of hours, he could not be sure which, hovering like ministering cherubim. Immediately behind them were serried ranks of textbooks in gray covers, flapping their pictureless, colorless leaves in unison. Old medical books with brilliant plates flew over, their leaves sodden, dripping from some recent shower. Close behind these were slim volumes of poetry in green limp leather, blue burlap or brown wrapping paper; Sankey was surprised to find these needed as much effort as the rest to stay aloft. Behind them fluttered beautiful loose-leaf cookbooks and gay picture magazines.

Here was all of literature, all of philosophy, all modern and ancient sciences, the sum of written thought. Sankey trained his binoculars on nearer titles that flashed by: Pascal's *Pensées* in a small indigo volume; Whitman's *Leaves of Grass* in olive green; *Rembrandt* in burnt umber; *Training the Collie* in white, and a small black pocket Bible. Here were the last living records of civilized man: almanacs, bank-books, address books, diaries, borrowed violet volumes from libraries. They fluttered and twinkled a thousand colors against the dimming sunlight (dimmed, he reminded himself, by other myriads like them): cheap paperback thrillers alongside *Tractatus Logico-Philosophicus;* Voltaire by Aquinas; Rabelais next to Elizabeth Barrett Browning.

And now the crowds below were holding up their volumes, spread face-down across their forearms, lofting them to the stinging wind. With a great, deep applause of clattering pages, these thousands of books rose to join the flock above.

'Wish we had something to send up,' Sankey shouted over the noise.

'Checkbooks! How about checkbooks?'

The two gray-haired men brought out their black checkbooks and solemnly flung them to the breeze. The thin, awkward things soared for a moment uncertainly, then began to flap their leathern wings with great energy.

'There must be something else,' Preston complained.

'Why not the draft of the report?'

'Why not? Who would want to read it anyhow, now: "A Report on the Migrations of Educational Materials".'

They lifted the half-completed draft from Preston's briefcase and balanced it a moment on the building's parapet. The spring clip at one side held the pages in a sort of book form, Sankey supposed. It might work.

'After you,' he said, stepping back.

Preston opened the batch of paper, lifted it like a shot putter and threw it straight out from the roof. It dipped, flapped shut and fell. Just as Sankey groaned, the bundle opened its wings once more, several floors below them, and began to fly.

It climbed fast, a magnificent patch of white against the dark cloud. Through the binoculars Sankey watched it join its brethren and turn itself toward the south. It was soon out of sight.

The Singular Visitor from Not-Yet, With an Account of the Subsequent Lamentable Decline of Dr Lemuel Jones

To Jeremy Botford, Esq.

Aug. 10, 1772

Dear Jerry,

It was with mixt feelings that I returned to London after all these years. The city is more splendid and horrid than ever; it is a sort of great Press, into which every kind of person has been tumbled, without the least regard for whether or not he is choaked with the stench of his neighbors.

For my part, the only retreat offering succour from the noxious Crowd's putrefaction is the coffee house. Of course I refer to Crutchwood's in Clovebelly Lane, which you may fondly remember. It still affords an entertaining company, and I was surprized to remark several of our old number about the fire yet. Augustus Strathnaver has grown quite stout and dropsical, but his Wit is lean and ready as ever. Dick Blackadder is still soliciting subscriptions for his translations of Ovid: he is still soliciting in vain: and he is still of good chear about it. I learned that poor Oliver Colquhoun, who never could get his play tried in Drury Lane, is dead.

But I was attended by the greatest astonishment when I apprehended a gross figure in a snuff-colored coat seated next the fire with its back to the company.

The figure turned to regard me, presenting its great warthog's face. When its mouth opened, 'twas like the splitting of a steamed pudding. 'So! [it said] I see you have not yet learnt your lesson, Timothy Scunthe, but must needs be taught more manners! Do you not know better than to interrupt a man while he is meditating?'

It was indeed our old friend, cantankerous as ever. I shall never forget the time I spilled mulled wine upon him—indeed, he shall never let me forget it, though it happened close on eleven years ago!

I stayed to see the evening out with Jones and his circle, to which there are no few additions. The good Doctor is thicker of limb, now, with a propensity (he says) to gout; though I perceive no shortening of his breath. He disposed last evening of two Philosophy Students (They were arguing about the Soul, I believe. I could not follow them), a Schoolmaster, a Grub Street writer, and a poor inoffensive solicitor who wandered in for a cup of tea and did not stay to see it cooled. In short, Dr Jones is himself: Witty, Splenetic and Eminently Sensible. I was keenly reminded of the days when we young dogs were used to teaze him, and he to muzzle us properly. Remember the fun we had with the visitor from 'the Future', and how the good Doctor shewed him for the merry Andrew he was? I can never forget it, as I hope you cannot forget

Your affectionate
Timothy Scunthe

To Sir Timothy Scunthe, Bart.

Aug. 25

Dear Tim,

I am glad you have not forgotten the Incident of the man from 'Not-Yet', for I have begun assembling some paltry Reminiscences and would greatly appreciate the help of your keen memory. While I believe I recall the Incident perfectly, much Muck has covered it in ten years' time, and I would rather have your version of the story, too.

Eternally gratefull, I remain, Dear Tim,

Your affectionate
Jer. Botford

To Jeremy Botford, Esq.

Sept. 5

Dear Jerry,

Your memory is doubtless better than mine, but I have made some Notations of that curious Incident, which, in the interests of your book, I hereby place at your disposal:

It was a December evening in 1762, and our usual circle, dominated by Dr Jones, was gathered in the gaming room at Crutchwood's. Pauceford, the proprietor, seemed to be having an argument with some man in the front doorway, and the room grew quite chill.

'Damme, sir,' Jones roared out. 'Are you determined to give us all the Ague? Bring the gentleman in.'

Pauceford led in a thin, splindle-shanked fellow, oddly dressed. I recall he wore his hair natural and shockingly short, and that his breeches reached to his ankles.

Jones' snuffbox clattered to the floor. 'Good God!' he cried. 'What manner of Whig is this?'

The fellow made no reply, but gazed about him in some consternation.

'Or is it Methodism you're spreading? Or Dissention?' Jones snarled. 'You'll do a barrel more converts if you bag a decent periwig.'

'Perhaps,' said Strathnaver, tittering, 'perhaps the gentleman believes it is Satanic to adorn the body.'

'Yes, well, you'll take note he has no scruples against hiding his spindly calves, however, My name is Dr Lemuel Jones, sir. You'll forgive me for not rising. I am rather gouty this evening. What might your name be?'

The man put out his left hand, withdrew it, then offered it again. Finally he extended his right and shook.

'My name is Darwin Gates,' he said shyly. 'And I'm from the Twentieth Century.'

Dr Jones' hand hesitated just a fraction as he reached for his snuffbox. 'Is it a place, then?' he said, offering snuff around. 'I should have thought it a direction. But it is very interesting to meet you, sir. I suppose you have all manner of wonders to divulge to this fortunate company, do you not?'

Mr Gates sat down and leaned forward earnestly. 'As a matter of fact, I do. You wouldn't believe the half——'

'Indeed? But I have a reputation for credulosity,' Jones said. A sly smile was beginning to play about his great, ugly mouth. 'You will want to tell me no doubt of carriages that operate without benefit of horses. Of engines that carry men through the air likes birds. Of ships without sails.'

The man flushed darkly and stammered, 'As a matter of fact——'

Jones' voice rose in both pitch and volume. 'Of machines which carry men under the waters of the sea like fish, where they witness countless wonders. Of mechanical horses capable of drawing a dozen carriages at once. Of artificial candles, powered by some mysterious force of which we know nothing as yet. Of buildings made of crystal and iron, perhaps, wherein one may order servants to select the weather one desires. Is that the sort of Future you are about to describe for us, Mr Gates?'

The poor visitor looked positively apoplectic with embarrassment and chagrin. I had no doubt but that he had planned a much poorer tale than this. 'I——' he stammered, '—that is, I——'

'BUT,' continued Dr Jones, grinding his teeth, 'I speak only of mere physical inventions, devices which any clod Mechanick may surmise. 'Twould do you no credit at all, sir, if you had not a better tale than this. Perhaps you come to tell me of the Politicks of the Twentieth Century. Let me see—there would be no war, because terrible Weapons would have been invented, the which are too dangerous to be used. The colonies in America will have rebelled and become a Powerful Nation, where, they will claim, All Men are Equal. Mayhap they will even free the slave Negroes, though that is perhaps too much to expect of our American friends.'

'Just a minute!' said the visitor. 'I resent that. I'm an American.'

'Tush!' said Jones. 'Next you will be a Red Indian. I warn you, sir, it was I who exposed George Psalmanazar, who posed forty years as a "Formosan", having made up his own "language".' All this Jones delivered in an undertone, then resumed his ordinary Rasp and said, 'I suppose the Powers and Alliances of all Europe will have shifted considerable. England's monarch will have no more weight than a common sweep, I suppose.'

'How did you know?' asked the astonished Mr Gates.

'Pooh, sir, I am merely spinning my tale to keep from being bored by yours. But be so good as to let me go on. I have not yet discoursed upon the Future state of Painting, of Musick, of

Moral and Natural Philosophy——'

'First we must give Mr Gates a cup of punch,' murmured Strathnaver. 'Assuming, that is, that persons from that time so little evident to our senses *can* drink and eat. Are you, Mr Gates, an aethereal spirit, like one of Mr Milton's angels? Do you sleep, ingest food, and so on?'

While the poor stranger was helped to a cup of punch, Dr Jones sat back and regarded him incuriously. I read contempt in Jones' face; whenever the right side of his mouth gets drawn up, as though attracted to the wart just above it at the corner, then he is in a phrenzy of contempt.

'Of Painting I know little,' he said. 'It is at best a clumsy art, making awkward imitations of Nature. I expect patrons will grow weary of Copyism, and turn their attention elsewhere.

'Everyone in the Twentieth Century will of course have Musick at hand as he desires it. I can well imagine the deleterious effect this will have upon Taste & Sense, when every cordwainer or every smith can hammer upon shoes to Musick of his own chuzing. Art does not, sir, lend itself to Dilution.

'There will always be a plethora of varieties in the Garden of Philosophy from which to make a nosegay. At some point, men will stop speaking of Reason and start speaking of Responsibility. There is, as they will say, no order in the Universe but what we chuse to see—as there were no Giants in Sir Quixote's windmills. Absurdity will become a philosophical catchword—there will be a Silly Season.

'Of Natural Philosophy I can well imagine the devising of all manner engines and games. No doubt men of the Twentieth Century will go to and fro the Moon, if not the Sun. Astronomy, Chimistry, Mathematics and Medicine will all advance space. Plague will be almost unknown. I daresay it will have been proven to everyone's satisfaction that Tobacco is a poisonous weed.'

'Amazing!' quoth our visitor. 'How did you know——'

'I have met better mountebanks than you, sir!' said Jones, fetching him a stern look. 'I am forced by gout to sit here night after night, prey to every single one of 'em. Only last month I was confronted by a "man from Not-Yet" who puts you to shame. Not only had he elegant manners and wondrous tales to tell, he looked exactly like me!'

Our visitor looked pale and ill. 'Like you?' he said.

'Yes. The rogue tried to convince me that he *was* me, but I have not yet met the man I could not outreason. I proved to him, as I shall prove to you, that man cannot travel from the Future to the Past.

'Man cannot move about in Time as though it were Space. Nature forbids it, as she forbids Levitation or a Vacuum. Think of the awful Paradoxes which might occur! Should you, for example, return to your childhood, you might see yourself as a child. Yet suppose your carriage ran over that child? Would you then cease to be? How then would you yet be alive? And there are Paradoxes even more hideous to contemplate. Suppose you got a child upon your own mother, and suppose the child were you? How then, may a man be his own father or son, a travesty of Physical and Moral Law? I do not even dare consider that weightier problem by far: Which of you, should you meet yourself, would have your Soul? Is the Soul single or divisible? Would some of your selves be soulless animals, mere Automata?

'You cannot be from the Future because the Future is, by definition, that which is not yet. There is no Future. And even were travel in time possible, you would not be from Posterity. I believe that Man grows every generation more happily endowed with Understanding—yet you are content to sit here gape-mouthed, listening to specious arguments.'

'Please,' said Mr Gates. 'I can prove I'm from the Future. I have built the only Time Machine ever. Let me prove it. Here is a coin——' He fumbled at the hip of his breeches for a moment. 'Here is a quarter of a dollar, United States of America currency,' he announced proudly, handing the coin to Strathnaver. 'You'll see the date is nineteen-something.'

'Good God!' said Strathnaver. 'The poor wretch has made himself credentials. This is no more a coin than I am. Hoho, Mr Gates, I must give you a lesson in minting, someday. When you design a die, you must *reverse* the image, so that it comes out proper on the coin.'

He passed the coin round, and we could all see that the inscription was backwards. It was poor forgery.

'Things have got reversed somehow!' shouted Gates. 'I don't know how. What can I do to make you believe me?'

'Nothing on earth,' said Jones. 'The last knave shewed me a curious engine he called a Lighter—but when I examined it, 'twas nothing but a tiny oil-wick lamp with a matchlock flint attached.'

'I'll take you back to my own time, and that will convince you!'

'A pretty idea,' said Mr Strathnaver, 'but you'll never get him away from the fire.'

'What?' said Jones. 'Quit the fire to wander about in the aguey snow until this rascal's fellows waylay me and kill me? I cannot say I like the prospect.'

'Oh, we needn't go far,' said Gates. 'My Time Machine is very close by—and some of your friends can follow and watch. Can it be you are afraid to prove me right?'

For once, Jones had no answer. He leapt up with surprizing agility and signalled for his cloak and hat. 'Let us see it, you dog,' he rumbled.

Dick Blackadder and I were elected to follow. We went but twenty paces in the snow when we encountered the 'Time Machine'. It was somewhat like a sedan-chair, somewhat like a bathing-machine and no little like an upright coffin on wheels. Gates opened a panel in it, and the two men got themselves inside. The panel closed up.

Dick and I watched the device closely, ready for any trick. All was deathly still.

'I fear something has happened to Lemuel,' said Dick. 'He could never keep silence this long.'

I wrencht at the handle of the panel, but it was fast. An unearthly light seemed to stream from crevices and cracks about the door, increasingly bright. I applied my eye to a crack and peered in.

There was not a soul inside.

The light got brighter and brighter until, with a thunderclap, the entire machine fell to pieces about me. I was knocked flat by the Great Noise, and when I regained my feet, I was amazed to see Dr Jones standing alone amidst the wreckage.

'Are you hurt, Dr Jones?' asked Dick, scrambling to his feet.

'No, I—No.'

'But where is Mr Gates?'

'It would seem,' said Jones, looking about, 'that he is blown into aeternity.'

We helped him back to the fireside, where, as I recall, he was strangely silent and morose all evening, and would not respond to no amount of badinage. He remained muffled in his cloak and refused to say a word.

That is all I know of the incident, Jerry. Hoping this account is of some good, I remain

Your affectionate
Timothy Scunthe

To Sir Timothy Scunthe, Bart.

Sept. 9

Dear Tim,

Rec'd your story and am truly amazed at the copiousness of your memory and notes. Surely you are more the man to pen a Reminiscence than I. You have captured nicely the flavour of the old Warthog's speach, and I find your account exact in nearly every Particular.

Do give my regards to Dr Jones and pray him to send me some little item of interest to go in my Reminiscences. If it would not inconvenience him, I would like mightily to hear more of his Experience that strange evening. Eternally gratefull I remain

Your affectionate
Jeremy Botford

Postscript. How is it you say the Doctor has a wart upon the *right* side of his mouth? I have before me a miniature of him, shewing the wart plainly on the *left*.

Yours &c.,
Jer. Botford

To Jeremy Botford, Esq.

Sept. 14

Dear Jerry,

Business is pressing. This is only a brief billet to inform you that I have spoken to Dr J. and he has promised to send you something. 'But I doubt (said he) that he will want to use it.' Do you understand this? I confess I do not. More later from

Your affectionate
Timothy Scunthe

To Jeremy Botford, Esq.

Sept. 15

My Dear Jeremy,

As you hold this letter up to a looking-glass to read it . . .
. . . I hope you will find it in you to pity its author. Do not, I beg you, judge me until you have read here the truth of my plight.

Having departed on December 10, 1762 from the yard of Crutchwood's, I journeyed into the Future. Having made my jokes about the Twentieth Century, I lived to see them, tragically, become Real. I saw Art & Architecture decline to Nursery Toys, and Literature reduced to Babel. Morality vanished; Science pottered with household Enjines. The main buziness of the time seemed to be World-Wide War, or man-made Catastrophe. Whole cities full of people were ignited and cooked alive.

Betwixt the two wars, people drive about the countryside in great carriage-enjines, which poison the air with harmful vapours. These carriages have o'erlaid the cities with smoak, black and noxious. There is in the Twentieth Century neither Beauty nor Reason, nor any other Mark which sheweth Man more than a beast.

But enough of a sad sojourn to a dismal place. I was sickened by it to near the point of madness. I knew I had done Wrong in accompanying Mr Gates to his Land of Horrors, and so I devized a plan for cancelling my visit.

I came back to November 1762 and saw myself. I earnestly entreated myself not to attempt such a voyage—but the object of this entreaty was so intent on proving me a scoundrel and imposter than my arguments were in vain.

I had then but one chance left—to appear at the time and place in which my unsuspecting self was departing for the Future, and to stop myself, by force if need be. Gates and poor Jones had just climbed into the Time Machine when I materialized. They disappeared at the same moment, and the combined Force of our multiple Fluxions destroyed the machine utterly. It was the first and last of its kind. I believe.

For some reason I cannot determine, I am reversed. Mr Gates thought that perhaps each Time-Journey reversed all the atoms of one's body. If you recall, when Gates first appeared, he kept trying to shake hands with his left hand. Likewise the coin in his pocket was backwards. In my journey to posterity, I was reversed. When I came back to speak to myself, I was put to rights again. Now I am again reversed.

You will not be able to include this in your book, I fear, unless as a Specimen of a madman's raving, or as a silly Fiction. Let it be a Fiction, then, or ignore it, but do not deride me for a Lunatic.

For I have seen the Future; that is, I have peered into the pit of *Hell.*

I pray you remain constant to
Your friend,
Lemuel Jones

To Jeremy Botford, Esq.

Sept. 15

Dear Jerry,

I have not yet time to answer your letter properly. I trust Dr J. has sent you or will send you his Reminiscence. I may say he certainly acts peculiar nowadays. I understand his demeanour has declined steadily over the past ten years. Now he is often moody and distracted, or seemingly laughs at nothing.

For example, he burst out laughing today, when I asked him his opinion on American taxation. He is an enigma to

Your affectionate
Timothy Scunthe

Postscript. Your miniature lies, for I have just today looked on the original. *My* memory may be faulty but my eyes are keen. The wart is on the *right*.

Yours, &c.,
T. Scunthe

The Short, Happy Wife of Mansard Eliot

Mansard Eliot's shadow, long with aristocracy, came out of his gallery on Fifth Avenue and moved along the sidewalk. Eliot knew exactly how he looked, with the sun gleaming in his hair. The hair would be parted slightly to one side, smoothed flat all over, and rich with dark, oily health. And the teeth: so white and even that Gladys said they reminded her of bathroom tiles.

Today he'd asked Gladys to become his wife. And if Dr Sky didn't like it, so what? Dr Sky, with his 'separation of dream life from reality', his 'horizontal cracks in the ego structure'! Let *him* try flopping down on the truth table like a seal pup and trying on the hard hat of memory ... Mansard would, by Heaven, marry beneath his station.

Today she was making up her mind. While he waited, Mansard recalled the formula for locating street addresses on Fifth Avenue. From 775 to 1286, he knew, one dropped the last figure and subtracted 18. It was just something like that, he supposed, some geographical or historical fact, that had made him rich. So today he had asked Gladys to divorce her husband, Dean, who was unemployed. As soon as she answered 'Yes', Mansard would rush away to tell Dr Sky.

'I can't divorce Deanie,' she whined. 'It would break his back.'

'I see.' Mansard was grave. His cereal company had founded a sports foundation, whose director was just now clearing his throat to make an announcement. Mansard Eliot owned at least one tweed sports jacket, one black or navy blue blazer, one sterling shoehorn, one pair heavy slacks, one summer suit, one drip-dry shirt, one raincoat, one pair cotton slacks, two neckties, two sportshirts, one pair dress shoes, one pair canvas shoes, one light bathrobe, three pairs of socks, three sets of underwear, two handkerchiefs, one bathing suit, toilet and shaving articles (adapted for European use), and the building in which Gladys was a scrubwoman.

'Deanie needs me,' she explained. 'People try to harm him. Yesterday I came home and found him sleeping on the couch, and the kids had put a plastic bag over his head. They hate his guts. He could have died. He hates their guts, too.'

What does Monique van Vooren do after dinner? A candle sputters. She fingers the bottle's long, graceful neck. Suddenly there is a shower of liquid emeralds. *Mansard was taller than Gladys, who, of Gladys, Mansard and Dean, was not the shortest.*

'He beats me,' she explained. 'He makes me have children I don't want. He doesn't want them either. He makes me go out and work, while he just lays around the house, guzzling two kinds of beer. My mother hates his guts. She'll be glad when I divorce him.'

The *Stallion* is a westernized shirt, extremely tapered, of cotton chambray. Why be bald?

'Everyone just hates his guts,' she explained. 'He even hates himself. Only I understand and love and cherish him. Or maybe it's only hate. Well, anyway, at least he loves his kids.' Minnesota has 99 Long Lakes and 97 Mud Lakes.

'Why don't we just pick up and go to Europe?' Mansard asked, glancing at himself in the lake. 'Or somewhere else?'

'Oh, I couldn't leave the kids. They don't get along with Deanie too well. They just don't get along.' Gladys put down her mop and pail and accepted a cigarette from the gold case he proffered. Satin sheets and pillow cases are a must for the compleat bachelor's apartment. The Doggie Dunit makes an ideal gift memento or 'ice-breaker' at parties. So realistic your friends will gasp. Mansard's hand trembled as he lit two cigarettes with a special lighter, then handed one to Gladys.

'Do you smoke?'

'Oh, no thanks. But you go ahead. I like the smell of a man's cigarette.'

Exhaling a cloud of aromatic smoke, he said, 'Let me think. now...'

She lit two cigarettes and handed him one. When he had

lighted their cigarettes, Mansard closed his eyes.

He consumed her with his eyes: her cold-reddened nose, print dress, feet swelling out of water-stained wedgies. His apartment, a penthouse over the supermarket, was filled each evening with soft Muzak. Alone at night, he'd listen, smoking one of his specially-blended cigarettes in the dark. The apartment could take her for granted; why couldn't he?

'How can you love him?' he said, touching his glass to hers. 'He even hates himself!'

But she would not speak. 'It's no good, our meeting like this,' she said, 'Mansard. Secret rendezvous in elegant nite spots. Dancing till dawn in posh cafés. Moonlit rides with the top down. Our own flower code. Losing a cool ten G's at Chuck-A-Luck and laughing like the crazy fools we are. "The wrong hotel room." *Billets-doux*. Smoking menthol by mountain rills. Appearing nightly in an exclusive engagement. Sailing. In fact, all water sports, including snow and ice as water. And finally, my love, leaping down a volcano, together.' She seemed unable to speak.

Mansard thought of Dean. Just place the International audio wall probe against any wall, and pick up sounds, voices, in the next room. Dual listening device, used by law enforcement officers on a world-wide basis, attaches to any phone. The Snooper—world's only private listening device, used by law enforcement officers, amplifies sound 1,000,000 times. Looks like a briefcase. Peeping Tom snooper scope is no bigger than a fountain pen, yet gives 6x magnification.

'I want to meet this "Dean",' Mansard said suddenly.

'So you want to degrade yourself,' said Dr Sky. 'Why, do you think? Has it anything to do with the time my father strapped me to my little potty chair?'

'His father did nothing of the kind,' said Mansard evenly. 'I never said he strapped me *down*, only strapped me.'

'Why did we feel trapped?'

'He did strappado me once,' said Mansard. 'He had some notion it would make me grow taller, have more confidence with tall women, business associates. As usual, he was right.'

'So we tell ourselves.'

Mansard recalled. 'He used to force-feed me. Vivisected my dog, to explain to me the mysteries of biology. Poor Spike.'

'Or poor you, you mean.'

'Yes, Dad never ceased preparing me for future happiness. He had a nurse read Kant to me while I slept. I had this recurring nightmare of being chased by a synthetic *a priori* proposition. I always wanted to go to Europe, but I never did.'

'What do you dream of recently?'

Mansard Eliot took down the dream in shorthand, a skill he'd learned in three short weeks. 'Last night I dreamed I was a member of a kid gang. We were beating a toilet with big chains. The sight of all that lavender porcelain being torn away made me sick, but I didn't dare let on.

'Then I was in the hospital, where the doctors were scraping pain or paint from me, using chisels and saws. It seemed to be the pineapple festival. I got up and ran down a hall lined with red formica. There were thousands of people all going to the big pineapple fire. I saw a man eating a doughnut made of ice cream, and I noticed it was a rose wreath from my grave. There was money all over the floor, and lucky charms, but it was electrified. I tore along on my scooter, whose headlamp seemed to show darkness instead of light. It was all tinker toys ahead of me, and cages full of live soap. I had to hurry, before the bureau closed, but the hands on my watch were wrong, no matter how I turned it to look at it.

'At the movie tent, the screen was blank, but everyone sat watching. "What is it?" I asked my mother, the projectionist. "See for yourself," she said. The x-ray glasses had some instructions written on them, on the cardboard bows, but in code. I deciphered it letter by letter: it was a letter from Monique van Vooren to Mamie van Doren, giving the menu. I ordered coffee eggs. They were beautiful, made of transparent plastic garden hose and film—but just then mass was starting. Father Zossima, Father Coughlin, Father Divine, Father Christmas, Father Flanagan, Father Keller and Father were officiating, but then I had to climb a windy mountain, strangely grown with hornets. At the top was—never mind.

'Hacking my way through the swamp, I went down into a subway station. All the trains ran to a place called "Breakfast". I started the engine with a huge, three-pronged key. Gladys and I sped along the highway, chased by a synthetic *a priori* proposition. They proposed to lock her away in a priory, see——'

'Time's up!' cried the doctor, waking to his wrist alarm. 'We'll take up there tomorrow.'

'But I haven't told you half of it! Then I was spearing——'

'I'm sorry, but I have another patient. Write it all down, we'll discuss it tomorrow.'

Mansard hid in a phone booth in the lobby, until he saw Dr Sky leave with his golf bag.

Dean was short, fat and altogether friendly-looking. For example, he wore a t-shirt with the message 'Thank God It's Friday', though it was only Wednesday. His arms were tattooed with Dumbo and Pinnochio.

'Navy?' asked Eliot, taking the initiative.

'No, I just wanted 'em. Who knows why kids do these crazy things, anyway.' Remove unwanted hair. Learn meat cutting: people must eat! Mansard noticed Dean had a faint, not unpleasant halitosis. *Robbed* of your high school diploma?

'So you're Glad's boss?' Dean, a bald, perspiring man whom Mansard Eliot had just met, laughed.

'That's right. She's told me so much about you, Mr——'

'Call me Dean,' Dean —— said. 'Want a beer? We got two kinds.'

Mansard decided it was time to speak. 'I think we can talk this over like civilized people, Dean.'

Dean smiled. 'Dalu 'mun karon fenna,' he said. 'Waa narrapart weearn manuungkurt barrim barrim tillit impando. Nxabo amacebo: amakwata nekra wai?'

'I want you to give Gladys her freedom.'

'So Glad tells me. It's sure okey by me. I'll miss the old sock, but——' He made a deprecating gesture, as if to say '*Mes sentiments!*'

Mansard took from his pocket a bullet. 'Glad to hear you take it like a man, Dean,' he said. 'So many men of your station—no offense intended—would have made a scene, screamed bloody murder, and so on.'

'I'm just curious, understand, but why do you want her?'

In the silence, Eliot's watch emitted a tiny electronic scream. Why did he want her? How to put it into words? He glanced over at her, sitting before the television with her feet up. Half her face was in shadow. From the other half, her hand removed blackheads at regular intervals, using a silvery plunger. He thought of the times she had refused to come to him, times when he'd rushed into the closet to press his burning face into a cool, damp mop, inhaling the sweet–sour fragrance of her. Her mop!

'One wearies of explanations,' he said.

'That reminds me, what about the kids?'

'I was thinking we'd send them to some sort of school or camp,' said Mansard easily. 'You know, nothing terribly expensive, but exclusive enough. We've written to Auschwitz, for one.'

Dean raised an eyebrow. 'Bet it's hell trying to find anything reasonable these days.'

'And how! Prices are absurd—it must be the administration.'

'Just what Glad was saying the other day. Her very words. I don't know what the country's coming to.' Dean's face grew red. He slapped the table, shouting, 'Damn it all to hell! It makes me sick the way the government pushes around the Little Guy!' Inside this pencil is a quality stapler! Inside this exact replica of a bottle of scotch is a 9-transistor radio that's on its way to being *the* executive gift! 24-kt golden peanuts contain lighter, pillbox, or executive toolkit!

'I couldn't agree more,' said Mansard. He opened a small, gold-filled penknife. Usually it was used to clip the ends from the cigars he had made up in Havana and flown in by special plane. Today, however, he put it to a new use, clipping off the bullet's nose.

'What's that you've got there, a bullet?'

'Yes, a *slug*.'

Dean opened two kinds of beer. 'I see you're making a dum-dum out of it. Neat idea.'

Mansard showed him the gun. Dean's eyes widened. 'That's a beauty!'

'Thanks. I call it my *gat*.' Eliot worked the action back and forth.

'I understand a forty-five is powerful as hell,' said Dean. 'Knock a man down if you only get him in the little finger. But how's the recoil?'

Mansard loaded and cocked the gun. 'Well, it seems big at first, but I've been practising.'

Gladys stood up as he sighted along the barrel at Dean's heart. 'No you don't!' she tittered, throwing herself in the line of fire.

A lady traveler to Europe should take: four pairs of nylon panties, six pairs of nylon stockings, two petticoats, two bras, a cardigan sweater, a pair of slacks or bermuda shorts, a pair of sandals, a pair of good, sturdy walking shoes, a pair of dressy heels, bathing cap and suit, one knit daytime dress, one drip-dry daytime blouse . . .

'Damn,' said Dean, looking down at the body. 'I'm really going to miss her. You notice how loyal she was—died trying to save my life—notice that?'

'Yes. I expect the police will be wanting this.' Mansard took from his pocket a personalized pencil with his name in gold, set of twelve, 60¢ ppd., inserted it into the barrel of the automatic so as to preserve his prints, and handed it over.

The Momster

They were letting him down easy. It was more humiliating, at least for Sewell, to be let down easy by a machine.

It leaned back in its swivel chair, looked above his head, and placed its plastic fingertips together. It feigned reluctance to speak.

'I'm sorry, Mr Sewell, but frankly we have our doubts. Your test scores ... I wouldn't like to say positively *no* at this time, you understand, but the outlook is bleak. Bleak.'

'I get the message. Don't Call Galactic Explorations, you'll call me.' Roger Sewell stood up. 'But I'd have appreciated getting the shaft from GX via a human interviewer, and not from a thing that looks human from the waist up only.'

'Wait.' The machine held up a hand wearing a military class ring. 'Wait, hear me out. It's this kind of behavior we might have expected, knowing your test scores. You must learn to deal with given reality, Mr Sewell.

'Now we'll submit your scores and application to the board, and their decision will be final. You aren't out of the running yet, unless you wish to be.'

Sewell wanted to step around behind the desk, grab the coax that formed the bottom half of the interviewer, and twitch it out of its socket, leaving 'him' frozen with that smarmy smile on 'his' face. But he also wanted to be an explorer, and there was only one way to get out there, through GX.

Therefore he remained seated, staring at a poster of an explorer with the usual equipment: cleft chin, white teeth, blond hair being rumpled by an alien wind, and far-seeing blue eyes. Three lightning bolts carried the message:

'IT TAKES GUTS.'

'IT TAKES IMAGINATION.'

'ARE "YOU" MAN ENOUGH?'

Behind him the interviewer cleared its throat. 'We'll be calling you, then, Mr Sewell.'

Whoever the board were (and he imagined a coven of humanoid mechanisms grinning and nodding at one another), they did finally approve his application. When he had signed his contract, things moved into high gear. In one day he was uniformed, innoculated and given a brief lecture on his destination, New Cedar Rapids. Early the next morning, he was transmitted.

He snowshoed the quarter mile of sand from the receiver to the main tent, wearing an oxygen mask and goggles. It was unpleasant just the same, slogging along. The wind was cold, flailing him with grit. By the time he'd arrived, he felt as if his neck and ears were bleeding, and his scalp caked with dirt.

Through his grimy goggles he saw two figures waiting to greet him inside the plastic tent, a man and a woman. It was only when he had got inside that Sewell realized the 'woman' was a machine. 'She' was of indeterminate age, slim, almost pretty, if you didn't notice the hinged jaw.

'Hi,' she said, shaking his dusty hand. 'I'm Rita, your partner here. This is Benny, the man you're rotating for some well-earned rest back home.'

Oddly enough, it was she who seemed spontaneous and alive, while Benny behaved like a run-down clock. He did not offer to shake hands, but only stared at Sewell for several moments; then turned and walked slowly away. He returned with a log book and pen.

'I'll sign out, then,' he said, looking hesitantly from one to the other.

'He wants you to sign in,' Rita explained. 'So he can leave.'

'For some well-earned,' said Sewell drily. He took the book and signed, wondering about the other man. Couldn't he have shaken hands or said hello? All right, he was tired, but——

'Goodbye, Benny,' the machine said. Benny mumbled a reply, slipped on the mask and stumbled away, not even looking at Sewell.

'Roger Sewell,' she read from the book. 'May I call you Roger?'

'Suit yourself. Where do I put my stuff?'

'I'll have to clean up Benny's quarters for you—it's a pigsty. Honestly, I don't know how you men can get that way, I really don't. I don't have an official name, by the way. My makers called me Rita, but my friends usually call me Mom.'

'Mom? Why?

'I don't know. A joke? Because that's what they need out here, maybe, a mom. Because they depend on me? I don't know.'

Sewell decided to call her nothing at all.

'Well, what are my duties going to be? What's the routine?'

She smiled. 'We can talk about that tomorrow. Right now I'll clean up your room, Roger, and then maybe you'd like to take a nap. You must be tired from your trip.'

He didn't like this. 'No, I'm not tired at all, as a matter of fact. And I'll clean the room myself, thank you.'

He did, and dumped Benny's miserable effects—dirty socks, a bent deck of cards, a comb fluffy with dead hair—into a plastic bag. He installed Jane's picture, his philosophy books, his journal. After making the bed, he sat on it, and prepared to meditate. The door slammed open.

'I thought you might like a nice cup of tea, Roger. I could have made coffee, if you'd preferred, but I was making tea anyhow and so I just thought I'd try it out on you. You sort of look like a tea man to me, I could be wrong, but usually I can tell a tea or coffee person just by looking at them. The only ones who ever throw me are the cocoa people, and thank God there aren't many of them. I don't know what it is, but I never have trusted a man who likes cocoa all the time, so you know what I mean? Oh, I know it's silly, but . . .'

He sat there, amazed, and watched her. She talked on about tea, about the different kinds, and the fact that they all come from the same plant, but from different parts of it, harvested at different times of the year. She spoke briefly of tea ceremonies, of which she personally knew nothing, she would be the first to admit, and of unjust tea taxes and the Revolutionary War. She went on, until the tea grew cold in the cup she was holding. Then she went back to the kitchen.

Sewell wedged a chair against the door. When he had

meditated for half an hour, he felt mildly euphoric, full of energy and ready to start work. The chair began to crack.

'Why have you got your door fastened? Roger, it's only me, bringing you a cup of tea. Roger?'

The chair splintered and in she came, beaming through the steam. As he drank the tea, she told him Benny and the others had always liked a cup of tea at about this time of day. Of course Benny was English, and liked his tea with milk. She preferred lemon, some nothing. Then there were catnip tea, camomile tea and mint tea...

Sewell finally stopped the flow by asking her about the work.

'Oh don't worry about that, not today. You just got here, for goodness sake. Take it easy.'

'I didn't come here to take it easy,' he found himself shouting. 'I came here to explore. Now are you going to tell me the set-up, or am I going to switch you off?'

'I'm sorry.' She was silent a moment, twisting her fingers in the ends of her apron strings. 'Roger, I didn't want to tell you this right away, but the fact is, there just isn't any set-up. There just aren't any duties for you.'

'What do you mean?' He leaped up and grabbed her by the throat. 'What do you mean by that?'

'It's true,' she said evenly. 'You can check the general rules bulletin, and the roster of back orders, clear back thirty years ago, when we first came here to Cedar Rapids.'

'I believe I'll do just that!' He slammed her against the wall and strode into the office. An hour later, when she brought him a sandwich and milk, he was sitting with his hands tangled in his gritty hair.

It was true. The first explorers had measured the planet, discovered its single mountain chain, examined the consistency of the sand that buried nearly everything else, plumbed the two lakes, tested their water, and recorded the weather.

Now, as far as GX was concerned, the work was finished. Daily weather observations and periodic examination of the sand could best be done by machines. A man would be stationed on New Cedar Rapids to keep GX's claim clear, 'just in case'. There was nothing for him to do, for two years.

'I think I'll go out and scout around anyway,' he said, later that evening. 'Where's the oxygen equipment?'

'Well—actually there isn't any, Roger. We haven't kept one here for years. There's just the one each new man wears, which the old man wears when he leaves again.'

'Damn!' He thought for a moment. 'I could probably get by with just an air filter, for a little while. I'll try that.'

The machine had begun baking cookies, and the tent was filled with the fresh smell. 'You'll have to get an early start, then,' she said. 'The wind gets too high later on.'

But he slept late the next morning, and when he awoke, it was with the luxurious feeling of playing hookey. This wasn't going to be so bad at all, he reasoned. There were a million worthwhile things he could fill his time with: there was his study of logical empiricism, which he could really get into, maybe even write a paper or two. There was his journal. All right, it wouldn't be a chronicle of adventure, but a record of his thoughts and impressions from the center of a sandstorm. He could write a novel. Finally, he could meditate. In fact, he could begin right now.

But first, breakfast in bed. She lingered in the doorway, asking him what he'd dreamed, commenting on the way he'd arranged the room. 'Is that your girl? "All my love, Jane." Isn't that sweet? Nice-looking girl, too. What they call photogenic. Some people never come out right in pictures, and others look much better than they *really* look, you know? I'll bet Jane is that type.'

'What about you, Rita-Mom? I'll bet you photograph just exactly the way you look *in life*, eh?' He chuckled, seeing the remark had hit home.

He tried to do some philosophy with what was left of the morning, but she interrupted him first to clean the room ('It's in the general regulations'), and again to ask him what he preferred for lunch.

Lunch was excellent, but the home-brewed beer that went with it made him sleepy. He dreamed of Jane, but the machine kept wandering into the dream at awkward moments. Then,

Jane, too, became a machine, and he discovered that, from the waist down, she consisted of nothing but a coaxial cable.

He awoke late in the afternoon, with a headache and an unpleasant taste in his mouth. Mom was there with the aspirin and lemon tea.

'I've wasted the whole day,' he said. 'It's getting dark.'

'You just aren't adjusted,' she said soothingly. 'The day only has twenty hours here, you know. I've never figured out why they stuck to the same old clock, instead of shortening the hours, and having twenty-four again. As it is, they have a fraction left over every day, so we gain a day every so many months. Or is it lose a day? I never can remember whether you set the clock ahead or behind, can you? It's the same with Daylight Savings Time . . .' And she was off, discoursing ignorantly on time for nearly one (normal) hour. It was only a machine, he told himself. He could turn it off any time.

He sat over his journal for four hours after dinner, but all he could write was:

'Sand. Sand. Sand.'

The following days were more of the same. His study of philosophy bogged down the day she showed him she could reel off pages and pages of Wittgenstein in German or English —and considered Wittgenstein a waste of time. He noticed he was putting on weight, then stopped noticing. Finally he hung a dirty undershirt over the mirror in his room, and forbade her to touch it.

She interrupted his meditations so often that he found them impossible even when she didn't interrupt. He stopped shaving, at first to annoy her, then for no reason at all. In her cleaning, one day, she knocked Jane's picture down and cracked the glass. He forbid her to clean his room any more, regulations or no.

He found her supply of home brew and got drunk, sitting at the kitchen table and listening to her endless chattering.

'Shut up!' he screamed. Seizing her by the shoulders, he shook her. 'Shut up, for God's sake!' And stopped her moving, plastic mouth with his own mouth. 'I want a woman,' he murmured.

Slowly but firmly, the steel rods in her arms pushed him away. As always, her expression was calm. 'Unfortunately, my manufacturers didn't forsee your need,' she said drily.

'What?' he grunted it, his flushed, uncomprehending face hanging over her. He had begun to list, slightly.

'I'm not a woman,' she said, pronouncing the words slowly and distinctly. 'I'm a Kewpie doll, Roger.'

He was on his knees, vomiting, and then he lay flat in it and went to sleep.

In the morning he wrote a second entry in his journal:

'We are all machines, or'

He lay the fiber pen down without capping it. The ink in it dried, and the page with the unfinished entry became dusty.

With a fine irony, he began to call her 'Mom'. It became a meaningless, habitual form of address.

He wanted to go out, into the sandstorm, just once before his replacement arrived. But he was afraid.

Mom was talking about Jane's photograph. 'I mean, since the glass is cracked anyway, and it really is silly to try to remember people from photographs, either you remember them anyway, or——'

He touched the switch at the lobe of her ear, and she became a statue. In the silence, he could hear her watch.

Tying a cloth over his face, he hurried out.

It was inhumanly cold. The faceless landscape around him lay dormant. It was the floor of some lifeless sea, cold, empty, frightening. With effort, Roger pushed himself away from the door and waded out a few steps.

Then the bleak wastes came to life, at the touch of the morning wind. Dunes began to blur and shift, and the light of the sun was dimmed. Roger's breath came harder.

What was he doing here? The wind was furious, now, trying to bury his legs, flinging sand at his eyes. A man could die here like a scream, unnoticed amid the senseless movement of the sand. Roger felt himself smothering. The door, only a dozen steps away, seemed now unreachable. He saw himself choking, dying, his lungs filling up with sand, flesh torn from his bones, the bones themselves rubbed to sand...

Roger stumbled inside and fell across his bed, coughing and cursing, the tears pouring from his sore eyes. It was some time before he realized with a shock, that he was having hysterics.

'They told me an explorer needs guts and imagination,' he wrote in his journal. 'It was a lie. An explorer must be a coward, afraid to do anything beyond strictly following orders. He must not be able to care about a woman, a set of ideas, or a way of thinking or feeling. He must deal only with the mundane, the day-to-day, the "given reality", as the interviewer said.

'I think GX was ingenious to think of using a Mom for each explorer, to help break him down to an efficient tool. He who lives with machines becomes machine-like, and now I see the title Mom is more than honorific. She is truly the mother of the mechanism Roger Sewell.'

It was clever of GX to provide her with a switch, he thought. As if he were able to switch her off for good.

'—else you don't. Well, I see you've turned me off long enough to go outside and come back in tracking up the whole place, as if I didn't have enough to do. You men! If there weren't any dirt, you'd invent it, I swear. Now what are you doing, burning your journal? What in the world for? We could have used the paper. I was just thinking the other day, if I had some paper, I could write down alternate menus for each meal, and you could just check off what you liked, instead of my having to bother you with a lot of questions. And have you accuse me of talking too much, I know that's what you think. At least I don't brood, my mind's an open book . . .'

1937 A.D.!

Picture, if you will, an inventor, working in his bicycle shop in 1878. His long hair occasionally falls in his eyes; he shakes it aside impatiently, flexes sinewy arms against the pull of a wrench, biting his lip with preoccupation. Now and then he may pause to sip some of the cool lemonade his widowed Mom has brought to him, sip and glance up at the picture of Sam Franklin on the whitewashed plank wall. *Early to bed and early to rise* ... he thinks. *A penny saved is a penny earned.* His serious brows knit, as he ferrets the last bit of truth from these proverbs.

Such an inventor was Emil Hart. He and his mother shared a small cottage exactly in the centre of the state of Kiowa. Their modest home was otherwise undistinguished except for a heavy mortgage, which the good widow hoped to reduce. Toward that end she knitted clever antimacmillans (lacy affairs designed to protect the tops of sofas and chairs from a then-popular hair grease called MacMillan's) and sold peafowl eggs. Emil augmented this meagre income by repairing bicycles and selling the FRIDAY EVENING POST (founded by Sam Franklin). Yet he knew fate intended for him a greater calling —inventor of the Time Engine!

One day Fenton Morbes, the town bully, stopped by. Seeing the great engine spread over the entire shop, he whistled with amazement.

'What'cher doing?' he asked.

'I'm only filing a bit of isinglass,' said Emil, shaking the hair from his eyes. He had no time to waste speaking to Morbes.

'I mean, what'cher building?' Morbes removed his bicycle clips and tossed them carelessly into a corner. They were made of costly aluminium, for he was rich.

Emil sighed. 'I'm building a temporal extrapolator,' he said.

'It will enable me to go into the future.'

The bully guffawed. 'Stuff!' he said. 'Nobody kin go into the future!'

With a knowing smile, Emil bent over his work. After fitting the piece of isinglass into a gear of peculiar shape, he set about attaching a pair of wires to a telegraph key.

Morbes flushed red about the nostrils of his broad, saddle-like nose. He was not used to being ignored. 'Stuff!' he exclaimed once more. 'Even if it works, this here engine won't bring in enough to feed your peafowls, let alone pay the mortgage when my Paw comes around to foreclose.'

'Foreclose!' said the young inventor, growing pale.

'Yep. You'd better have a hundred dollars ready by next Monday,' said Morbes with a grin. 'Tell you what. If you'll wash my bicycle, I'll give you a whole dollar. Get it spanking clean now, for I'm to go on a picnic today, with Miss Maud Peed.'

At this news, Emil grew even paler, and staggered back as though he'd been struck.

'Oh, I know you been kinda sweet on her,' smirked the bully. 'But she ain't got no time for a crazy feller what putters around his bicycle shop with time engines. Hah!'

No time for him! As the colour continued to ebb from Emil's face, and into the coarser features of his rival, he wondered what strange fate it was that had made them both suitors for the hand of the lovely Maud Peed. So be it. He raised his tear-filled eyes once more to the portrait of Sam Franklin. He seemed to draw strength from the homely features, the rheumy eyes. What was the right thing to do, the truly *Columbian* thing? To try to stay and win Maud back from Fenton Morbes—a hopeless task? Or to escape into the bright future, and there seek his fortune?

In a moment he had made his decision. He would go into tomorrow! He would see 1937 A.D., that promised land—the very system of numbering our years promised it! He would drink in its wonders: flying machines, the bridge across the English Channel, immortality through mesmerism, electric cannon, a world at peace, where the sun never set on the flag of the United States of Columbia!

'Are you gonna stand gawking at that pitcher or are you gonna wash my wheel?' demanded Morbes.

'Neither. You may take yourself off my property at once,' replied Emil. Raising his clenched fists, he added, 'Go to Maud Peed. And tell her—tell her——'

His hands dropped to his sides, and as his head bowed, the unruly lock of hair fell over his eyes. He looked not unlike the young Abner Lincoln, thought Morbes idly.

'—tell her,' Emil said quietly, 'that the best man has won. I wish you both a—haha—a happy future!' With a strangled sob he turned away.

Morbes was so startled by this outburst that he was unable to summon a bluster to his lips. He turned and walked out.

Emil knew he had done the right thing. Without another regret, he filled his pockets with his Mom's home-baked cookies, took a last sip of lemonade, and began to pedal the great generator that powered his engine. He had mounted a special clock face on the handlebars before him, and when its hands reached 1937, he depressed the telegraph key. 'Now it is

1937 A.D.!' he exclaimed, and looked about him.

The room had not changed considerably, though it seemed to have become some sort of museum. Emil found himself surrounded by velvet ropes.

'Here, get of there!' said a man in uniform. He seized Emil's arm and dragged him away from the time engine. 'You're not to touch the exhibits, understand?'

Before the bewildered inventor could explain, he found himself outside the shop, looking up at a brass plaque which read, 'The Emil Hart Historical Museum'. He was historical!

Pausing only a moment to marvel at his fame, Emil strode toward the main street of town, eager to see the changes time had wrought. The streets, he noticed, had a new hard surface, and there was not a trace of manure upon it!

Then he saw them, lined up at the sidewalk. Great trackless locomotives, just as he had imagined them. As he watched, two men emerged from a store and entered one of them.

Through its window he could see one man shovelling coal into the boiler while the other turned valves. In a moment, the great, chuffing engine moved off down the street.

His momentary elation dissipated at once, when Emil turned to look at the shops. There was not a single new building on Main Street, and though many had installed large plate glass windows, the facades above them were faded, dirty and abused. Delmonico's Dining Room had become the Eateria, but Carlson's Peafowl Feed Store had not even changed its sign. Emil examined the contents of a clothing store window, his gorge rising at their dull familiarity. Why weren't people attired in seminude costumes of gold, with scarlet capes? The mannikins showed only women in the same silly hats and long gowns, men in dark, dull suits. Worse, the one or two pedestrians he glimpsed wore overalls of the same cut and hue as his own.

He was thoroughly depressed by the time he reached the end of the town's single street and the Public Library. Despairing of seeing any more wonderful inventions like the trackless locomotive, Emil made his way into the familiar building to the tiny room marked 'Science and Technology'. Here at last he might find respite from the past. Here he might find the future that seemed to have overlooked his town.

He opened a volume marked 'Inventions'. Yes, here they were: Thomas Elva Addison, the electric light; Burgess Venn, the flying machine; Gordon Q. Mott, the televidium—what in the world was that?

He looked it up in the back of the book, and learned that it was a visual counterpart to the radium. The latter sent verbal messages over long distances by means of electrical 'waves' in the aether, while the former did the same for visual messages. He thrilled to the idea of electrical waves moving about everywhere, in this room, passing right through his body. It was only because of the intensity of Emil's meditation that he failed to notice the figure at his elbow.

'Hullo, Emil.' It was Morbes.

'You used my machine?'

'Yep. I came back to get my bicycle clips and I seen you

was gone. Well, I got to thinking—a feller could make himself a pile of money outa knowing what happens in the future. So here I am. Where do they keep the old newspapers?'

'What are you going to do?' Emil leapt to his feet, knocking over a chair. Another reader cleared his throat.

'Read about a few horse races—and some stock market stuff. I'm rich now, Emil Hart, but I'm gonna be richer.' Morbes's grin displayed a row of uneven, stained teeth.

'You can't! It's dishonest! Think of all the little stockholders who might be ruined by your speculations!' cried Emil. He followed the bully into the Historical & Periodical room, and seized his arm. Morbes shook his hand away.

'Leave me alone!' he bellowed. 'I'll do as I see fit!'

'Yes, do leave him alone!' commanded a childish voice. 'I'm trying to read here, and you're creating a disturbance.' Emil looked around to confront a boy of about ten, whose forehead was creased with annoyance beneath the line of his yellow bangs.

Grinning, Morbes said, 'Lad, where's the newspapers? You know, the WAAL STREET JOURNAL?'

'I don't know. All they have in here is this.' The boy indicated the volume open before him, in which he had been scribbling with a pen. Emil noticed it was one of a large matched set that seemed to occupy all the shelves of the room. There were thousands of volumes.

'But this will have whatever you're looking for,' said the boy. 'It has a synopsis of everything.'

The set of books was entitled *The Universal Synopsis*.

'Say!' exclaimed Morbes, illuminated by an uncharacteristic flash of intuition. 'If I get rich like I ought to, there should be something about *me* in that book.'

He searched a moment, then came to the table with volume MORAY-MORBID and seated himself opposite the boy.

'Here it is! Morbes, Fenton Jr,' he read at the top of his lungs.

'Don't read on!' said Emil. 'We're not meant to know our own futures.'

'Stuff! Who's to stop me?'

'I am!' Emil shouted, and snatching up the boy's pen, dipped it and lined out the passage Morbes was about to read.

'Say, why'd you do that? I——'

With an audible click, Fenton Morbes vanished.

'How interesting!' said the boy. 'I was right, then. This *is* the only extant copy.'

'What?' Emil stood frozen, gaping at the space his rival had vacated so abruptly.

'You don't know what happened? That was the "Doppler Effect", named for myself, Julius Doppler. Sit down, won't you, and I'll explain it to you.'

Emil eased himself into a chair and with effort directed his gaze toward the serious, freckled face.

'You see, I've developed a theory that the future influences the past. I was fortunate in finding *The Universal Synopsis* on which to test it. If this were, as I believed it to be, the only copy of the only book in which many items appeared, why then it follows that I can change the past by merely rewriting it.'

'But how can you change history?' asked Emil, mystified.

'It's simple semantics: The word *is* the thing—at least after the thing ceases to be. Alter a word in the future and you alter the thing it once stood for. Let me show you.'

The boy opened his volume to a page and pointed. 'Now here, I altered the name "Sam Franklin" to "John Franklin", for example. But if in the future, someone came along and changed it to—say—"Ben", why he'd *be* Ben, don't you see?'

'No.'

'All right, look here, then.' Julius turned to a map of the United States. There was the familiar pink lozenge that was Kiowa, and just above it, the green hourglass of Minnehaha—but the names were wrong! 'Kiowa' missed its 'K', and Minnehaha' read 'Minnesota'! And the name at the bottom of the page, following 'The United States of' was not 'Columbia' but some unpronounceable Latin name! The map was wrong, it had been printed wrong!

'Last week,' said the boy, 'I made these changes in ink. Now this week they are part of the original book.'

'But how can that be?'

Julius frowned. 'I think the past must influence the future, too,' he said. 'But the influence is *slower*. My theory is really quite a simple one, but I couldn't possibly explain it to *you*, not all of it. Why, you don't even understand $e=mc^3$, for Pete's sake.'

'I understand one thing,' said Emil, leaping up. 'I know that I *killed* poor Morbes! I am a murderer!'

'Don't take it so hard,' said the boy. 'You wouldn't have, if it weren't for me. In fact, the only reason you're a time-traveller is because I wrote the whole thing in the margin near your name.'

'My name?' Emil was electrified at this reminder of his fame. 'My name . . . Won't you have a cookie?'

'Thanks.' The two of them munched Widow Hart's cookies and discussed the theory once more, until Emil was sure he understood. He was not so sure he liked being at the mercy of the future, but when one considered it, it was no worse than being at the mercy of the past. One survived.

When the last cookie was gone, Emil rose and took his leave. He strolled back to the museum and paid his admission. After a few moments, he was able to seize an opportunity when the guard was not looking and leap upon his time engine. He pedalled furiously backward to 1878, and what a glorious feeling mounted in his breast as he gazed once more on the homely feature of John Franklin.

'I *am* healthy, wealthy and wise—or shall be shortly,' Emil told himself. 'My rival is gone—I don't even remember his name—and I am to be famous!'

After changing to his Sunday clothes, he picked a nosegay of his Mom's flowers and set off toward the Peed house.

Mr Peed was seated in the porch swing, industriously polishing his pipe against his nose.

'Hallo, young Hart,' he called out. 'What brings you out this evening, all dressed up like that?'

'I——' Emil began, then realized he did not know the answer. Why *had* he come to see Mr and Mrs Peed?

'Flowers for your wife,' he decided aloud. 'From Mom's

garden.'

'Whose wife?' asked Peed, leaning forward to accept the nosegay. 'I ain't married, son. I——'

Peed's outstretched hand grew transparent. Then Peed, porch and house vanished with a click.

It was a nightmare! Emil hurried home to check on his Mom. There was no telling who might click out of existence next!

He was reassured by the sight of her frail old figure tottering into his shop with a tray.

'Here, let me take that,' he said, and accepted the tray from her careworn hands.

'Lemonade and cookies—for me? Gee, you're good, Mom!' He bent and kissed her white hair. With a beatific smile, the old lady tottered back to her kitchen, whence came the smell of fresh baking. Fearfully, Emil watched until she was out of sight.

He cornered Julius in the library and demanded an explanation.

'Of what?' asked the youngster. 'An explanation of what?'

'I'm not sure, but I think the Peeds had a daughter, and I think I was in love with her. Now she's gone, and they're gone—have you been eating again?'

'You did it yourself, pal. When you crossed out the reference to Fenton what's-his-name, you also destroyed the only existing reference to the girl, Maud. She was his wife. You got any more cookies?'

'You mean I'd have lost her in any case?'

'Uh-huh.' With his mouth full of the widow's cookies, the boy explained. Destroying Maud had destroyed her parents, their parents, and so on, back to the time when some relative was famous enough to have appeared in *The Universal Synopsis*. It was difficult for Emil to follow, for not only did the boy speak with his mouth full, but neither he nor Emil could clearly remember who it was they were discussing. As Julius said, it was all very mythical—or perhaps he said mystical.

At last, Emil was brought to understand he had lost the only girl he'd ever loved. His grief was superb.

He knew it was all his own fault. If only he had not wanted to glimpse the golden towers and battlements of the future! If only he had been content! His sin was pride, pride that goeth before (or, according to Julius, cometh after) a great fall.

What had she been like, this girl he'd lost? He had some faint reminiscence of her lovely eyes being hazel—or else her hair—or was it her name? In despair, he put his head on his arms and wept unashamedly.

'Here, read this,' said Julius Doppler. 'It'll cheer you up.'

It was the volume HART–HARUSPEX, and in it, Emil read:

'Hart, Emil (1860–?), inventor of the time engine and only successful time traveller. Leaving 1878 he journed into 1937, where, in a public library, he met *Julius Doppler* (q.v.), who explained to him the famed "Doppler Effect"—the influence of the future upon the past. After several blunders, Hart finally read his own story in *The Universal Synopsis* (q.v.), and realized as he did so that, had he read it earlier, he might have avoided making a costly mistake, the deletion of some probably mythical woman from history. As he realized all this, Hart is reported to have said, "Thunderation! Why didn't I think of this before?"'

'Thunderation!' said Emil, smiting his forehead 'Why didn't I think of this before?'

He referred not to his past mistakes, however, but to his successes yet to come. Borrowing the pen from Julius, who had just changed the peafowl to a chicken, Emil wrote in the margin the following:

'Nonplussed, the stout-hearted inventor re-created his girl, Hazel Peid, from memory, adding her to his life story. After a brief courtship, they married. The plucky Hart went on to become healthy, wealthy and wise.'

After a moment of thought, he added:

'And nothing anyone writes here in the future will ever make it otherwise.'

Then, giving Julius the last cookie, he departed.

She was there in his shop, the lovely Hazel Peid of the hazel hair and eyes—just as he remembered her. Going upon one knee, and tossing back his unruly lock, Emil said, 'Miss Peid, will you be my wife?'

'Oh yes!' she exclaimed, clapping her small, well-formed hands together.

'This calls for a celebration,' said Mom, tottering in with a tray. 'Won't you have some lemonade and cookies?'

Emil and his fiancée embraced, while above them the rheumy eyes of Ben Franklin seemed to smile a blessing.

My Indian valet, Oxbox, brought me a mint copy of *Ô*, the rare Dadaist book by Jean-Claude Odeon, long out of print.

'This is an unexpected treat, I can assure you,' I said, opening it to page forty-seven. I happened to know that, although the entire book consists of the letter 'ô' repeated fifty-one times to the line, twenty-nine lines to the page, for four hundred fifty-three pages, *genuine* copies possessed a certain typesetter's error. Sure enough, the third vowel on page forty-seven had no *accent circonflexe*.

'This single error,' I explained to Oxbow, 'means the difference between one of the rarest books in existence and a cheap fake worth but a few dollars. This book is genuine.' I tore out page forty-seven and ate it, washing it down with *Guardia Civil*, a liqueur distilled from Ovaltine. 'But who could have sent it, Oxbow?'

'I do not know, *boss-wallah*,' he said. 'It come by special messenger few minutes ago, in plain wrapper.'

I snapped my fingers. 'I'll bet it was Margo!'

'That right, *kimo sabe*. I never think of that.' My valet scratched his head with bewilderment. Then, divining my wish, he fetched me a telephone on which to call my friend and 'companion', the lovely Margo, and ask for a date.

'Aw gee,' she said. 'I was just gonna wash my hair.'

But I would not be put off. 'Margo, you lovely, lovely creature,' I breathed into her receiver.

Before we arrived at the party, Rose Garland, that still-young Gold Star mother, said: 'Think of it, Brad! Six million Jews!'

'Not exactly.' Brad, her still-handsome husband, smiled tolerantly. 'You forget that, with all their reputation for efficiency, the Germans were notorious bookkeepers.'

'Notoriously bad, you mean?'

'Ah, who can say what is bad?'

The garbage under Mrs Onager's sink grew, slightly.

Rose was reading, and Brad was watching her read. He had already finished the 'Gordimer' trilogy, by P. B. X. Thomson: *Gordimer's Chance, Gordimer's Fate* and *Gordimer's Folly.* Now he waited for guests with whom to discuss them. They might also discuss *novel,* a novel by Horace Mattrick, the guest of honor. Mattrick had not yet arrived. Fenster Doybridge had not even been invited.

On the kitchen floor, Gene said no to Eileen.

Many years earlier, when I had lived in Greenwich Village and worn oxford shoes, my Hispano-Suiza had inadvertently been ticketed for overparking.

Gene got up and went out to a Civil Defense meeting. Tad crept in and took his place.

'Why is it they call you "Tad"?' Eileen asked.

My Hispano-Suiza was now at the garage, having a special type of bazooka mounted under the bonnet. Wrapping a white silk scarf about my throat, I squeezed through a panel at the back of my medicine chest and climbed to the roof. My Nieuport was there, already throbbing with life.

'Keep an eye on things, Oxbow,' I shouted over the throaty roar of her engine. 'I may not be back until morning.'

'Can do, *sahib*!'

'And don't forget to feed Black Phantom, my wonder dog.'

'Roger, *baas*! Later.' He saluted smartly.

I lifted the Nieuport's nose starward, and then, levelling out, kicked her around in the direction of Margo's penthouse.

It was back in Greenwich Village I'd met Sunspot—and of course his girl, Waverly, who was naturally bald, and favored suedehair bathing caps.

With the autopilot on, I used my superior powers of concentration to read, in quick succession:

Your Earning Power, by M. Bartleby.

Colitis, by Duane Gardens, M.D.

A Treasury of Fire Myths. O. Dawson Lotts, ed.

Speaking of Those Darned Kids, by Pete Lamb
Lesbians Unaware, by Duane Gardens, M.D.
Raising and Training the Apache Indian, by D. Gardens.

Peering over the side, I beheld a short dark man observing me through binoculars, but thought nothing of it at the time. I felt in no immediate danger from the ground, having fortified my plane with one of my earlier inventions, bullet-proof air.

I found a note on Margo's door: 'Have gone to Paris for a few things. Have *not* been abducted.' *Not* abducted? It seemed oddly worded to me. Could this be a case of protesting too much? Margo certainly did know her Shakespeare. Or could this be a trap of some kind? I determined to follow her, after a few drinks.

Gene, whom I then knew as Jean-Claude, had defended me at the trial. The Hispano-Suiza, the ticket, and the entire section of street were brought in as exhibits.

At the Hotel Odeon, the U.S. Army Poets' Convention was having a reading, so I stopped there for my drink. A fat boy named Pfc Lyle was just reading the end of his epic *Japaniad*. I tried to make my way through the crowd to have a word with him in private, but found my path blocked by a giant specialist.

'Go to!' he cried, breaking a beer-bottle. Using a trick I'd learned in the Orient, I applied pressure to the base of his thumb until he was unconscious. The crowd of rude soldiers parted to let me pass.

I found Pfc Lyle alone at a table, weeping and drinking. Another infantryman had taken the platform to read a poem called 'Ingredients'.

'Hello. Pfc,' I said. Lyle looked up.

'You!'

Meanwhile, at a party for Vance Raglan, someone—possibly Doybridge—was speaking: 'A book, or else a film. Yes, I think it was called ... or is it the record I'm thinking of?'

Vance Raglan was a sculptor in glue. Eileen thought of the Orient, of her Buick dealer, of Thomas Hardy's latest novel. She thought of throwing a 'Famous Mac' party. To Tad, she said, 'Goodbye, Tad, or whatever you call yourself now. I'm off to Hong Kong.'

She shook hands with Doybridge—a mistake.

'Sunspot,' I said, and Pfc began to weep again. I truly felt like weeping with him, but, for various reasons, my tear ducts had been removed. Sunspot! Our old companion, now dead or missing. Sunspot! Who claimed to be a preincarnation of Moondog. Sunspot! Our best friend at obedience school.

Pfc clutched my sleeve and croaked, 'Hey, remember how he always used to claim it was him did the whining on the sound track of *Lassie Come Home*?'

On the platform, the soldier read, '... milk solids, soya meal, gum arabic, dried eggs, powdered yeast, corn starch, dextrose, maltose, monosodium glutamate, artificial flavoring and coloring. Sodium propionate added, to retard spoilage.'

Amid the wild applause, one radar specialist asked another: 'I think it lacks something, don't you?'

'I remember Sunspot,' I said, my voice husky with remembrance. 'When I was living in the Village, he'd come over while I was out and leave a little memento in the middle of the floor.'

'According to the legend, he was run down by a car he was chasing. Later, sharp operators all over the country began selling plaster replicas of his "little mementos" in novelty stores.'

'He never saw a dime of millions they made.'

Taking my leave, I flew direct to Le Bourget airport at Paris. As I had no passport, the immigration officials tried to stop me, thus forcing me to flash my special identity card. At the sight of it, they waved me through the gate with profuse apologies.

The garbage beneath Mrs Onager's sink began to stir.

I knew exactly where to find Margo. She was at Les Halles, bargaining with a merchant. Margo's French, as always, was flawed, so the poor man had difficulty understanding what it was she wanted—eggs to wash her hair.

'D'ozene,' she said, making a sign, 'pour mes chevaux.'

Exasperated, the man asked me why Mademoiselle's horses should require putrid ulcers of the nose.

When I'd bought eggs for Margo, we flew back to a party for Plastic Man. On the way, we stopped off at the flower market in Barcelona, where I bought a sprig of bloodslipper for her hair.

'Gee thanks.' She pushed it among the pink curlers, making them look quite festive. We jestingly argued about the relative merits of the French language and the language of flowers.

In Hong Kong Eileen gave the plague to a number of people. The plague was tularemia, commonly called 'rabbit fever'.

'Plas' was playing a game of hide-and seek with a number of distinguished guests, among them the brilliant arachnologist, Dr Aa, various crowned heads and pretenders, including the Prince J—— C——, and Mr Boggs, (Eileen's Buick dealer). Plas had already concealed himself as a lampshade, a comic book, socks, margarine, wallpaper and the yellow fog that rubs its back upon the windowpane. Now he was again hidden. Strangely, no one but me seemed to have caught on to the obvious deficiencies in his disguises, viz., he was always red, with black-and-yellow stripes, no matter what his shape.

I had several drinks and examined Plas's curious collection of medieval harrows. Tularemia, I recalled, was named after a county in California.

'One-two-three for Mr Boggs's cummerbund!' I called out suddenly. Smiling sheepishly, Plastic produced himself. I noticed, however, that his smile was a trifle lop-sided. Indeed, his whole head seemed to flow into fanciful shapes. I signalled Margo to get my scarf and her riding cloak.

'What's wrong?' she asked, as we hurried away to Mattrick's party. Dr Aa elected to come with us.

'Plastic was drunk,' I said harshly. 'That could have turned into God's own orgy.'

'Oh, you!' She seemed piqued but pleased.

Dr Aa made a suggestion. 'Why don't you leave the Nieuport here, and fly over with me in My Gee Bee Racer?'

We took him up on his kind offer. On the way, he explained to us why he'd left the Famous Mystery Scientists Club.

'It all began when I left my usual work to devote some time to a private investigation of gravity. By fractional distillation of cats, in the presence of your bullet-proof air, I managed to isolate a leadlike substance which is actually *repelled* by the attraction of earth! The farther it gets away from a planet, the greater is the repulsion.

'At great expense, I constructed a demonstration, but my colleagues were in league against me. "Fakery!" scoffed one. "Madness!" sneered a second. "Mesmerism!" insinuated a third.

'I was forced to return to my old occupation, arachnology. Now I work for the armed forces, classifying spiders "edible" and "inedible". I am *dead*.' He performed an Immelmann turn, by way of demonstration.

'That isn't the worst,' he continued. 'Foreign powers, chiefly the Finns, are now trying to steal my invention. I've been invited to play blindfold chess tonight at the party, and I fear it is there that an attempt will be made upon my life. Here——'

He pressed a scrap of paper into my palm. 'Here is the only copy of my formula. Take care it does not fall into the wrong hands.'

'It's safe with me, doctor,' I assured him, as I tucked it into a secret compartment of my billfold.

In Hong Kong, Oxbow caught tularemia. He was resuscitated by spleen massage, and as soon as he was able, called me on the radio.

'Did you feed Black Phantom, my wonderdog?'

'Yes, master. *Bwana*, take great care. Watch out for girl from Iowa Writers' Conference, *effendi*. Over and out, chief.' Just before he went off the air, I heard scuffling sounds—and a shot.

'He sounds a little sick,' said Margo. *She and Oxbow are the only ones who know my secret identity*. We disembarked at Mattricks' party, while Eileen, returning from Hong Kong, asked 'George' to marry her.

'To whom?'

A number of people seemed to be at the wrong party. Among these were a boy in a sleeper suit carrying a tire and a candle, a black-hatted quaker, a fat, jolly-looking Negress with her hair tied up in a red-and-yellow checkered kerchief, and a very tall green man. Their speech was strained, and I detected something familiar about the quaker's voice. Margo took down everything he said:

kodel fiberglas doelon polymite acrylan
curon durastran lastex vinylite fortrel
nykon polyester corfam fabricon acrylex
doron bunalenex lucite actinene creslan
dynel protofoam banlon caprolan formica
rayon celustran chemex fiberfil actinel
lurex quiltacel antron koromite spandex
nylon strantron forlon koratron polynel

Gene returned from his Civil Defense meeting, unslung his binoculars and asked Eileen what was new.

'Nothing much. Tad dropped in.'

'Why on earth do you call him "Tad"?' asked Gene.

A man in farmer costume came from upstairs to borrow some toothpaste. 'We're having a "Famous Mac" party,' he explained. 'I'm "Old MacDonald". Can I borrow some toothpaste? You see, we're all brushing each other's teeth.'

I walked over to Mattrick, who was engaged in conversation with a portly man in pince-nez.

'Hello!' said Mattrick. 'Didn't expect to see *you* here. Have you met Fenster Doybridge, the famous kidnapper?'

'We've met,' snapped the fat man.

'Indeed,' I said, offering them cigarettes. 'In fact, I saw a bit of your work this evening, if I'm not mistaken, Doybridge.'

He chuckled non-committally, and turned away to watch a Xerox engineer doing funny imitations. Suddenly I realized that Margo was nowhere in sight!

The man from upstairs came back for more toothpaste. 'It's taking a little more to finish off "Mary McCarthy",' he explained. 'Afterwards, we're gonna do some pantomimes. "Cardinal MacIntyre" is gonna harrow Hell for us, so "MacAdam" can build a road across it, on which "MacArthur" can return to the Philippines. Hope you folks don't mind a little noise.'

'Are you going to read from *novel*?' I asked Horace Mattrick. He nodded. 'I'd better. It's written,' he added, laughing, 'entirely in vowels—you're supposed to improvise the consonants—so most people have a little trouble with the plot.'

I watched the quaker make an odd sign to a tall, peculiar-looking man. This person wore only black sleeves and trouser legs over his thin limbs, his only other garments being a black stovepipe hat and a monocle. I remarked to Mattrick that the man looked like nothing so much as a half-naked peanut.

This peanut-man in turn made a secret signal to another man in a stovepipe hat (were they coming into fashion?). That man sported a wisp of white beard, but otherwise resembled a laborer, for his sleeves, blue with white stars, were rolled high on veinous, knotty arms. His hat was striped red-and-white.

I kept one eye on the girl from the Iowa Writers' Conference, who reeled from room to room in some sort of drunken dance. The phonograph was playing code. I noticed Doybridge listening closely to it, along with the men in the stovepipe hats.

And Doybridge had donned a stovepipe hat!

It was of black silk, to complete his costume of cutaway coat, striped trousers and spats. He carried a walking stick, and a bag marked with a dollar sign. As I stared at it, I realized with a shudder that *it was exactly the size of a human head.*

Stirring, the garbage under Mrs Onager's sink took on an unearthly shape.

'If I should marry you, Pater will cut me off with a penny,' said 'George' to Eileen. According to Eileen's way of thinking, *George* in French was *Georges*, while *penny* was pronounced to rhyme with *penis*. But Eileen was feverish, feverish and ill.

I wandered into the garden, where the quaker was behaving oddly with a tree.

'Sunspot!' I cried. 'Is it you?'

'Shh! The Finns or someone are tailing me. It might be only a joke, you know—a case of the wag tailing the dog—but don't let's take chances. Pretend not to know me, and for your own protection, go back inside.' With misgivings, I obeyed.

In one corner of the living-room, the Xerox engineer was

doing a clever imitation of a legal tort. In a second, Doybridge expounded an aesthetic of kidnapping. In a third, Eileen had curled up to read *The Renaissance,* while in the fourth, Dr Aa was just preparing to play blindfold chess with a short, swarthy man I recognized as Gene. I took it all in at a glance, not liking the look of any of it.

Fenster D. pontificated: 'In essence as in theory, in execution as in conception, from the first symbol to the ultimate sensibility, the whole must be, how shall I say ...'

There was an enormous CRACK! and the bedroom ceiling, bearing a man on a Mack steamroller, descended upon the pile of coats and on the girl from the Iowa Writers' Conference, and on Tad.

'It never happened before,' said the driver, who wore both a mackintosh and a mackinaw. A *deus ex mackinaw?* I wondered. It would do to keep a close watch on the 'Cardinal'.

Knowing that Dr Aa would open with a knight, his opponent had substituted for it a tiny, live, venomous seahorse. When poor Aa touched it, the creature bit him savagely.

'Aa!' Screaming his own name, the blindfolded arachnologist rose from the game and fell dead.

Mrs Onager peered beneath her sink and rubbed her eyes in disbelief.

As soon as the police left with Aa's effects, the girl from Iowa began her dance all over again.

'I have an announcement to make,' she sang. 'I'm not what I seem. Actually I came here to interest all of you in NAME LABELS. They are gummed for easy affixing to any surface, and they have YOUR NAME, YOUR ADDRESS, ANYTOWN, EVERYWHERE. One hundred cost only one dollar, and they come in this elegant styrene carrying case.' She exhibited a perfect little styrene box. Then, bending to trail her long, blonde hair, she swept about the room, taking orders for NAME LABELS. Seeing through her ruse, I vowed to deal with her later, after Mattrick's improvisation.

Opening his novel, *novel,* the famous author read:

'I did sit in Rimini, sipping drinks within its limiting light. In hip, with-it Rimini, I, light-tickling, kiss Mimi's lips. Isis

Mimi swings, I swirl, twirl this nitwit girl, fling digits in Rimini's wind, O Finns!

'O gold moon of Hong Kong! How now, brown orb of loot? Go to! Spook who glows or god who bows to boon, do not tow two old clocks on sloops or spoons on ponds (pools) of bold rococo. Row on row of cold wood brooms! Oxbow, London fog!

'A yak at last, a llama, half-mad after, alas, pasta, asks all that wash aft, madam. Man has castaway what cats ask. Ah, sad, mad, glad, bad tanks! Last act, Aa! Dallas!

'He never left the deck. We never held the end. The red shed never seemed free, we've seen. Bled green, he fed her eggs, beets, beef; he fed her greed. Never kneel! Well-met, Gee Bee!

'Up busts Luck. Run tub, bub. stuck-up ducks upchuck mud mukluks. Run, nun! Turds pluck up trust, sub fucks up, truck U-turns. Numb trust cuts guts. Ubu's pus must run, but . . .'

I drew my weapon as we applauded.

'Where could all that garbage have gone?' Mrs Onager mused. 'It couldn't have just *walked away*.'

Eileen began to feel as though she were coming down with psittacosis, commonly known as 'parrot fever', as she explained to Gene.

'Where did you get it?' he demanded jealously.

I shot the so-called girl from the fictitious Writers' Conference twice. I was just turning the body over with my toe when Marge came in from the garden, with Jean-Claude Odeon and Oxbow. We linked arms.

In the garden, Sunspot gave one strangled scream. Then all was silence, save for the stealthy, rustling, retreating step of the garbage man.

The Transcendental Sandwich

'We can give you knowledge,' said the salesman-thing.

Claude Mabry looked all around his room: mildewed wallpaper, broken linoleum, dirty long underwear slung over a chair that had a weak leg, the clock face that had been cracked and repaired so many time with scotch tape that he could hardly see it said 3.20.

'I'm smart enough for me,' he said. 'There's such a thing as being too smart for your own good.'

'That's right,' said the salesman-thing, 'and there's such a thing as being so smart you have to wash dishes down at Stan's Chili Bowl to earn enough to live—here.'

Claude could not reply. The whole thing reminded him of the Bible: a snake or whatever it was dressed up like a man, offering 'knowledge'—it just didn't make sense.

'Look, I don't mean to be unpleasant,' said the salesman. 'But we Guzz are a hell of a lot more powerful and a hell of a lot smarter than your species. If we'd wanted to, we could have vaporized your whole planet—but it's not our way. So when somebody comes offering to make you smart, don't knock it.'

Claude wanted to rip off that grinning, false mansuit and see what the Guzz looked like. He half-rose, then sank back again and looked at the floor.

'If you're so good, why do you want to do anything for me?'

'I don't want to do anything for you. I voted to turn Earth into a bird refuge. But we have a democratic form of government and the majority wanted to make your kind fit citizens to share the universe with us.'

'All right, how do I know you can make me smart?'

The salesman opened his briefcase and took out a handful of bright brochures. 'Don't take my word for it that we can make you one of the smartest men on Earth,' he said. 'Don't take it from me that being smart is worthwhile. Millions are trying our plan. Thousands have tried it already. Have a look.'

He handed Claude a folder showing full-color pictures of quiet scholars, white-coated scientists, dignified judges and beaming businessmen. Their testimonials were capped with red headlines:

COULD'T READ OWN NAME—
NOW COMMANDS 20 LANGUAGES!

FAMOUS ECONOMIST
'HATED ARITHMETIC'

'DUMB OX'
TO BRILLIANT THEOLOGIAN—IN 7 MONTHS!

'But—what would I study?'

'Everything.' The salesman produced another slick booklet and began turning the pages, showing Claude pictures of happy housewives and hairy-handed laborers reading heavy volumes, farmers peering through microscopes and grannies using slide rules. 'We call our system the Interface Way. Every person we accept must study at least two subjects intensively. If the subjects are unrelated, all the better. We mix mathematics with literature, we throw theoretical physics at a medical specialist, we give the mathematician theology.'

'What would I get?'

'If we accepted you, you'd be tested. Then we'd know.'

'What do you mean, if?' Claude felt he had just been offered a million-dollars, but at the word 'if' it had shrunk to about a nickel.

The stranger, sensing his anxiety, spoke soothingly. 'Don't worry too much about that. We won't be testing your I.Q. or previous knowledge. In fact, the less of either, the better. We want people who haven't had a chance, people who feel useless because the sleeping genius within them has never been awakened. What do you say?'

'I don't know. What would it cost me?'

'All the money in the world couldn't buy you a better education, pal. But all it costs is your signature.'

'Well—oh hell, why not?'

'Why not?' echoed the salesman, handing him a pen. Claude signed a few forms in various colors and the salesman gave him a copy of each.

'Claude,' he said, 'you've just made your first intelligent decision.'

The Guzz had pretty well taken over Earth, in every way. Guzz-developed gadgets were in every home. Clergymen thanked the Lord from their pulpits that the Guzz were not warlike or vicious but a truly democratic—ah—people. The government made daily announcements of new Guzz gifts to humanity.

They quietly disarmed the nuclear powers, they made efficient clean-air and sewage-disposal systems for our cities, they introduced new food sources and birth-control plans in Asia. Hardly a government bureau in the world had not been approached by the Guzz with a suggestion or a gift—and these aliens used no stronger forces than tact and kindly persuasion.

The only disagreeable thing about them was the way they looked—both at home and in Earth-drag.

On their own planet (or so it was said, for no one had yet visited them) the Guzz were disagreeably vermiform. Here, so as not to spook the natives, they wore human forms of plastic. Their movements in these were natural enough, but they all looked alike. As far as most people, including Claude, were concerned, the Guzz were just so many talking store-window dummies.

The first box that arrived was a table-top computer equipped with keyboard, microphone, speaker and visual display screen. That night when he returned from Stan's Chili Bowl, Claude lay awake looking at all that gleaming, complicated junk and wondering if he might have made a mistake in even hoping . . .

Next day three packages arrived. The first contained books

and a sheaf of documents: a certification that Claude Mabry was eligible for this correspondence course, more copies of the various forms he'd signed—and a booklet entitled: *Welcome, Future Genius!*

'The government of Guzz and your own government wish to take this opportunity to welcome you ... conditions and by-laws.... You may not always see the reasons for instructions given you in this course, but they are necessary to ensure efficient use of your time.

'The enclosed books are for Lesson One. The books required for each lesson will be provided with the lesson. At various points in the program you will be asked to study them thoroughly.'

Claude glanced at the titles of the books: *The Interpretation of Dreams,* Sigmund Freud; *Verbal Behavior,* B. F. Skinner; *Towards Information Retrieval,* Fairthorne; were only a few.

The dream book looked interesting but inside, like all the others, it was full of long-winded sentences that didn't mean anything.

The second package contained a tape cassette titled: *Program for Lesson One* and simple instructions for loading it into the teaching computer.

As soon as Claude could do so, he switched on the machine. He might have expected it to give him a problem, to register the fact that it was turned on, or at least to ask his name, but it did none of these things.

Instead, it politely requested him to eat a sandwich.

Claude scratched his head. The Guzz had to be joking. He could imagine them watching him right now, laughing at his stupidity. So this was the big learning course! So this...

He remembered the third package and tore it open. Inside was a cellophane-wrapped sandwich. Though Claude turned it over and over, he could see only one difference between this and any other cellophane-wrapped sandwich: Inside the wrapper was a plain printed name slip. But instead of 'ham and cheese' or 'peanut butter and grape jelly' it simply read:

Eat me.

The bread was a little stale but he enjoyed the salami or para-salami inside.

An hour later he correctly answered a request to explain how and why dreams were subject to syntactical rules. The answer was obvious.

Two hours later he had read Ayer's *The Problem of Knowledge*, read it at skimming speed because it was already perfectly familiar to him.

A lesson or two later Claude had gone through about fifty difficult books without any trouble. He progressed rapidly through the programs, though it did not seem like progress at all: he simply knew what he was doing. Using Fourier analysis to solve problems in electronics seemed something he had always known, just as he had always realized the gross truth of Newtonian mechanics and the finer truth of quantum mechanics, the position of Hubert Van Eyck in Flemish painting, the syllogistic properties of an Andrew Marvell poem, the flaws in the historical theories of Spengler and Toynbee—or for that matter, how to prepare *sauce ozène* with seven ingredients. Scraps of learning, areas of learning, even whole complex structures of learning were suddenly his.

Having learned, he worked. By the fourth lesson Claude had gone through Gödel's proof of the necessary incompleteness of mathematical theorems and picked holes in Lucas's application of this to mechanical devices. He had also put forth an aesthetic theory understandable by perhaps ten men, refutable by no more than one. He had nearly destroyed mathematical economics, and devised a tentative translating machine. He was hardly aware that these things had not been done before, nor was he really aware of the transition from his job at the Chili Bowl to a research fellowship at a prominent university.

The transition came about from his publication of various monographs in journals, the names of which he knew only from footnotes in the books he was skimming. Some of the monographs came back. He had sent them to wrong addresses, or to journals long out of print.

Others, like his 'Queueing Theory Applied to Neural Activity' and 'On Poetic Diction', became classics. Men with tweedy manners but sharp suits and clean attaché cases came to see him. They sat in the steamy, oily kitchen of Stan's Chili Bowl and talked with him about quasar explanations, new codes of international law and logic mechanisms. True, many prodigies were springing up now that the Guzz offered their massive home study program. But for the time being, genius was still something universities fought over. And so, almost without knowing it (he was thinking of other things), Claude Mabry gave Stan his notice, packed his T-shirts and blue jeans and entrained for Attica University.

He remembered only isolated facts about this trip: sending a change-of-address card to the Guzz; losing his ticket; not bringing enough paper (and so alighting from the train at Attica, where University officials were waiting to greet him, his hands so full of slips of toilet paper on which were penciled notes toward a theory of history that he could not accept the handshakes of these venerables). Without comment he settled into his new life and went on working.

From time to time he wondered what was in the sandwich that came with each lesson. A wonder drug that unlocked hidden knowledge that lay 'sleeping' within him? An intelligence accelerator? Whatever it was, it was essential to the process. The only time he'd tried studying without it, Claude had floundered among symbols that *almost* made sense.

He wondered, too, about the Guzz. The little he learned about their planet and culture (in the final lesson) whetted his appetite for more. He longed to know everything about them, almost to become one of them: They alone would understand what he was doing. It was becoming clear that his colleagues at the university considered him some kind of freak—he would not wear a suit, he could not converse about departmental politics and he was inhumanly intelligent.

Claude ordered all the information on the Guzz he could get. This proved to be a slim volume by a second-rate anthropologist who had interviewed a few of the aliens. Claude skimmed it and began a treatise of his own.

'Despite the advanced "democracy" of the Guzz,' he wrote, 'they retain a few oddly "primitive", even sacramental habits.'

There was a knock at the door. The standard face of a Guzz looked around the frame, saw that he was alone and walked its standard body into the office. Without saying anything, it came over and struck him on the forehead. Twitching, Claude slipped to the floor. The visitor busied itself with a set of plastic bags.

The fallen man was muttering. Bending lower, the man-shape heard: '... planarian worms? D.N.A. or... ?'

'Right you are!' boomed the Guzz. 'Yes, we *are* analogous to your planarian worms—so, of course, are you—and we can transmit behavior genetically.'

He fished a long knife from one bag and tested its blade against a false thumb. 'Of course our genes need help. Obviously our—I mean to include your—children do not learn much from their parents' genes. But these same genes, properly assimilated——'

'I knew it!' Claude croaked, getting up on one elbow. The blow had stunned him, but still the machinery of his mind ground on. With an ecstatic expression he said, 'The old taboos against eating the king, eating the old man, the sage, the father, yes?'

'Check.' With a hearty chuckle the visitor kneeled by Claude's side and felt for the carotid artery. 'Those ridiculous taboos have kept your species back hundreds of thousands of years. We're just now making up the lost time for you.'

'The sandwich meat——'

'Housewives, mechanics, professional people—all the people in that brochure you saw. Just think of it!' He waved the knife oratorically, and the plastic face turned up, as if gazing at a vista. 'One genius provides three thousand sandwiches, each capable of providing—with no wastage—part of the education for one more genius! Thus learning will transform your whole species—you will become as gods!'

The Guzz returned his attention to the matter at hand. He poised the knife.

'Superman,' murmured the genius. 'On white or rye.'

Capt. Charles Conn was thinking so hard his feet hurt. It reminded him of his first days on the force, back in '89, when walking a beat gave him headaches.

Three time-patrolmen stood before his desk, treading awkwardly on the edges of their long red cloaks and fingering their helmets nervously. Capt. Conn wanted to snarl at them, but what was the point? They already understood his problems perfectly—they were, after all, Conn himself, doubling a shift.

'Okay, Charlie, report.'

The first patrolman straightened. 'I went back to three separate periods, sir. One when the President was disbanding the House of Representatives, one when he proclaimed himself the Supreme Court, one when he was signing the pro-pollution bill. I gave him the whole business—statistics, pictures, news stories. All he would say was, "My mind's made up."'

Chuck and Chas reported similar failures. There was no stopping the President. Not only had he usurped all the powers of federal, state and local government, but he used those powers deliberately to torment the population. It was a crime to eat ice cream, sing, whistle, swear or kiss. It was a *capital* offense to smile, or to use the words 'Russia' and 'China'. Under the Safe Streets Act it was illegal to walk, loiter or converse in public. And of course Negroes and anyone else 'conspicuous' were by definition criminals, and under the jurisdiction of the Race Reaction Board.

The Natural Food Act had seemed at first almost reasonable, a response to scientists' warnings about depleting the soil and polluting the environment. But the fine print specified that henceforth no fertilizers were to be used but human or canine excrement, and all farm machinery was forbidden. In time the newspapers featured pictures of farmers trudging past their rusting tractors to poke holes in the soil with sharp sticks. And in time, the newspapers had their paper supply curtailed. Famine warnings were ignored until the government had to buy wheat from C****.

'Gentlemen, we've tried everything else. *It's time to think about getting rid of President Ernie Barnes.*'

The men began murmuring among themselves. This was done with efficiency and dispatch, for Patrolman Charlie, knowing that Chuck was going to murmur to him first, withheld his own murmuring until it was his turn. And when Chuck had murmured to Charlie, he fell silent, and let Charlie and Chas get on with their murmuring before he murmured uneasily to Chas.

The captain spoke again. 'Getting rid of him in the past would be easier than getting rid of him now, but it's only part of the problem. If we remove him from the past we have to make sure no one notices the big jagged hole in history we'll leave. Since as the time police we have the only time-bikes around, the evidence is going to make us look bad. Remember the trouble we had getting rid of the pyramids? For months, everyone went around saying, "What's that funny thing on the back of the dollar?" Remember that?'

'Hey, Captain, what is that funny thing——?'

'Shut up. The point is, you can change some of the times some of the time, and, uh, some of the—look at it this way: Ernie must have shaken hands with a million people. We rub *him* out, and all these people suddenly get back all the germs they rubbed off *on* him. Suddenly we have an epidemic.'

'Yeah, but, Captain, *did* he ever shake any hands? He never does any more. Just sits there in the White Fort, all fat and nasty, behind all his F.B.I. and C.I.A. and individualized anti-personnel missiles and poison germ gas towers and—and that big, mean dog.'

Capt. Conn glared the patrolman down, then continued: 'My idea is, we kidnap Ernie Barnes from his childhood, back in 1937. And we leave a glass egg.'

'A classic?'

'A *glass egg*. Like they used to put under chickens when they took away their children. What I mean is, we substitute an artificial child for the real one. Wilbur Grafton says he can make a robot replica of Ernie as he looked in 1937.'

Wilbur Grafton was a wealthy eccentric and amateur inventor well known to all members of the time patrol. Their father, James Conn, was an employee of Wilbur's.

'Another thing. Just in case somebody back in 1937 gets suspicious and takes him apart, we'll have the robot built of pre-1937 junk. Steam-driven. No use giving away the secrets of molecular circuitry and peristaltic logic before their time.'

The four of them, and a fifth patrolman (Carl) arrived one evening at the mansion of Wilbur Grafton. To the butler who admitted them, each man said 'Hello, Dad,' to which their unruffled father replied 'Good evening, sir. You'll find Mr Grafton in the drawing-room.'

The venerable millionaire, immaculate in evening clothes, welcomed them, then excused himself to prepare the demonstration. James poured generous drinks, and while some of the party admired the authentic 1950s appointments of the room —including a genuine 'stereo' phonograph—others watched television. It was almost curfew time, and the channels were massed with Presidential commercials:

'Sleep well, America! Your President is safe! Yes, thanks to I.A.M.—individualized anti-personnel missiles—no one can harm our Leader. Think of it: over ten billion eternally vigilant little missiles all around the White Fort, guarding his sleep and yours. And don't forget—there's one with YOUR name on it.'

Wilbur Grafton returned, and at curfew time, one of the men asked him to begin the demonstration. He wheezed with delight. His glasses twinkling, he replied: 'My good man, the demonstration is already going on.' Pressing one of his shirt studs, he added, 'And here is—The Steam-Driven Boy!'

His body parted down the middle and swung open in two half-shells, revealing a pudgy youngster in knitted swim trunks and striped T-shirt, who was determinedly working cranks and levers. The boy stopped operating the 'Grafton wheeze-laugh' bellows, climbed out of the casing, took two steps and froze.

'Then where's the real Wilbur Grafton?' asked Chuck.

'Right here, sir.' The butler put down a priceless Woolworth's decanter and pulled his own nose, hard. Clanking and creaking, he parted like a mummy case to give up the living Grafton, once more flawlessly attired.

'Must have my little japes,' he wheezed, as the real James came in with more drinks. 'Now, allow me to reanimate our little friend for you.'

He inserted a crank in the boy's ear and gave it several vigorous turns. With a light chuffing sound, and emitting only a hint of vapor, the small automaton came to life. That piggish nose, those wide-spaced eyes, that malicious grin were familiar to all present, from Your President Cares posters.

As the white-haired inventor stooped to make some further adjustment at the back of its fat neck, 'Ernie' kicked him authentically in the knee.

'Did you see that precision?' Wilbur gloated, dancing on one leg.

The robot was remarkably realistic, complete to a frayed strip of dirty adhesive tape on one shiny elbow. Charlie made the mistake of squatting down and offering Ernie some candy. Two other patrolmen helped their unfortunate comrade to a sofa, where he was able to get his head back to stop the bleeding. The little machine shrieked with delight until Wilbur managed to shut it off.

'I am confident that his parents will never notice the switch,' he said, leading the way to his workshop. 'Let me show you the plans.'

The robot had organs analogous to those of a living being, as Wilbur Grafton's plans showed. The heart and veins were really an intricate hydraulic system; the liver a tiny distillery to volatilize eaten food and extract oil from it. Part of this oil replenished the veins, part was burned to feed the spleen's miniature steam engine. From this, belts supplied power to the limbs.

Digressing, Wilbur explained how his grandfather, Orville Grafton, had developed a peculiar substance, a plate of which varied in thickness according to the intensity of light striking it.

'While grandfather could make nothing more useful of this "graftonite" than bas-relief photographs, I have used it (along with mechanical irises and gelatine lenses) to form the boy's eyes,' he said, and pointed to a detail. 'When a tiny image has been focussed on each graftonite 'retina', a pantographic scriber traces swiftly over it, translating these images to motions in the brain.'

Similar levers conveyed motions from the gramophone ears, and from hundreds of tiny pistons all over the body—the sense of touch.

The hydraulic fluid was a suspension of red particles like blood corpuscles. When it oozed to the surface, through pores, these were filtered out—it doubled as perspiration.

The brain contained a number of springs, wound to various tensions. With the clockwork connecting them to various limbs, organs and facial features, these comprised Ernie's 'memory'.

Grafton let the plans roll shut with a snap and ordered James to charge the glasses with champagne. 'Gentlemen, I give you false Ernie Barnes—from his balloon lungs out to his skin of rubberized lawn, fine wig and dentures—an all-American boy, made in U.S.A.!'

'One thing, though,' said the captain. 'Won't his parents notice he doesn't—well, *grow*?'

Sighing, the inventor turned his back for a moment, and gripped the edge of his workbench to steady himself. A solemn silence descended upon the group as they saw him take off his glasses and rub his eyes.

'Gentlemen,' he said quietly, 'I have taken care of everything. In one year's time, this child will appear to be suddenly stricken with influenza. His fever will rise, he will weaken. Finally I see him call his mother's name. She approaches the bedside.

' "Mom," he says, "I'm sorry I've been such a wicked kid. Can you find it in your heart to forgive me? For—for I'm going to be an angel from now on." His eyes flutter closed. His mother bends and kisses the burning forehead. This triggers the final mechanism, and Ernie appears to—to——'

They understood. One by one, the time patrol put down their glasses and slipped silently from the room. Carl was elected to take the robot back to 1937.

'He was supposed to bring the kid here to headquarters,' said Captain Charles Conn. 'But he never showed up. And Ernie's still in power. What went wrong?' A worried frown puckered his somewhat bland features as he leafed through the appointment calendar.

'Maybe his timeer went wrong,' Chas suggested. 'Maybe he got off his time-bike at the wrong place. Maybe he had a flat—who knows?'

'He should have been back by now. How long can it take to travel fifty years? Well, no time to figure it out now. According to the calendar, we've all got to double again. I go back to become Charlie. Charlie, you go back to fill in as Chuck. Chuck becomes Chas, and Chas, you take over for Carl.' He paused, as the men exchanged badges. 'As for Carl—we'll all be finding out what happens to him, soon enough. Let's go!'

And, singing the Time Patrol song (yes, they felt silly, but such was the President's mandate) in deep bass voices, they climbed on their glittering time bicycles, set the egg-timers on their handlebars and sped away.

Carl stepped out from behind a tree in 1937. The kid was kneeling in his sandpile, apparently trying to tie a tin can to a puppy's tail. The gargoyle face looked up at Carl with interest.

'GET OUTA MY YARD! GET OUT OR I'LL TELL ON YA! YOU HAFTA PAY ME ONE APPLE OR ELSE I'LL——'

Still straddling the time-bike, Carl slipped forward to that Autumn, picked a particularly luscious apple, and bought a can of ether at the drugstore. Clearly it would take both to get this kid.

'I spose,' said the druggist, 'I spose ya want me to ask ya why you're wearing a gold football helmet with wings on it and a long red cape. But I won't. Nossir, I seen all kinds...'

In revenge, Carl shoplifted an object at random: a Mark Clubb Private Eye Secret Disguise Kit.

Blending back into his fading-out self, Carl held out both hands to the boy. The right held a shiny apple. The left held an ether-soaked handkerchief.

As Carl shoved off into the gray, windswept corridors of time, with the lumpy kid draped over his handlebars, it occurred to him he needed a better hiding place than Headquarters. The FBI would sweep down on them first, searching for their missing President. A better place would be the mansion of Wilbur Grafton. Or even ... hmmm.

'An excellent plan!' Wilbur sat by the swimming pool, nursing his injured knee. 'We'll smuggle him into the White Fort itself—the one place no one will think of looking for him!'

'One problem is, how to get him in, past all the guards and ——'

Wilbur pushed up his glasses and meditated. 'You know the President's dog—that big ugly mongrel that appears with him in the Eat More Horsemeat commercials—Ralphie?'

Compulsively Carl sang: 'Ralphie loves it, every bite/Why don't you try horse tonight?'

'I've been working on a replica of that dog. It should be big enough to contain the boy. You dispose of the real dog tonight, after curfew, then we'll disguise the boy and send him in.'

When the dog came out of the White Fort to organically fertilize the lawn, Carl was waiting with the replica dog and an ether-soaked rag. Within a few minutes he had consigned the replica to a White Fort guard and dropped Ralphie in the dim, anonymous corridors of time. No one need fear Ernie's discovery, for the constraints of the dog-shell were such that he could make only canine sounds and motions.

Carl reported back to the mansion.

'I have a confession to make,' said the old inventor. 'I am not Wilbur Grafton, only a robot.

'The real Wilbur Grafton invented a rejuvenator. Wishing

to try it, without attracting attention, he decided to travel into the past—back to 1905, where he could work as an assistant to his grandfather, Orville Grafton.'

'Travel back in time? But that takes a time-bike!'

'Precisely. To that end, he agreed to cooperate with the time patrol. On the night he demonstrated the Steam-Driven Boy, you recall he left the room and returned wearing the James-shell? It was I in the shell. The real Wilbur slipped outside, borrowed one of your time-bikes, and went to 1905. He returned the bike on automatic control. I have taken his place ever since.'

Carl scratched his head. 'Why are you telling me all this?'

'So that you might benefit by it. Using your disguise kit, you can pose as Wilbur Grafton yourself. I realize a time-patrolman's salary is small—especially when one has to do quintuple shifts for the same money. Meanwhile I have a gloriously full life. You could slip back in time and replace me.' The robot handed him an envelope. 'Here are instructions for dismantling me—and for making the rejuvenator, should you ever feel the need for it. This is a recorded message. Goodbye.'

Why not, Carl thought. Here was the blue swimming pool, the 'stereo', the whole magnificent house. James, his father, stood discreetly by, ready to pour champagne. And the upstairs maid was uncommonly pretty. It could be a long, long life, rejuvenated from time to time . . .

Ernie sprawled in a giant chair, watching himself on television. When a guard brought in the dog, it bit him. He was just about to call the vexecutioner, to teach Ralphie a lesson, when something in the animal's eyes caught his attention.

'So it's *you*, is it?' He laughed. 'Or should I say, so it's *me*. Well, don't bite me again, understand? If you do, I'll leave you inside that thing. And make you eat nasty food, while I sing about it on TV.'

'Poop,' the child was thinking, Ernie knew.

'I can do it, kid. I'm the President, and I can do anything I like. That's why I'm so fat.' He stood up and began to pace the throne room, his stomach preceding him like a front wheel.

'Poopy poop,' thought the boy. 'If you can do anything, why don't you make everybody go to bed early, and wash their mouths out if they say——'

'I do, I do. But there's a little problem there. You're too young to understand this—I don't understand it all myself, yet—but "everybody" is you, and you're me. I'm all the people that ever were and ever will be. All the men, anyway. All the women are the girl who used to be upstairs maid at Wilbur Grafton's.'

He began explaining time travel to little Ernie, knowing the kid wasn't getting half of it, but going on the way big Ernie had explained it to him: Carl Conn, posing as Wilbur, had grown old. Finally he'd decided it was time to rejuvenate and go back in time. Fierce old Ralphie, still lurking in the corridors of time, had attacked him, and there'd been quite an accident. One part of Carl had returned to 1905, to become Orville Grafton. Another part of him got rejuved, along with the dog, and had fallen out in 1937.

'That Carl-part, my boy, was you. The rejuvenator wiped out most of your memory—except for dreams—and it made you look all ugly and fat.

'You see, your job and mine, everybody's job, is to weave back and forth in time——' he wove his clumsy hands in the air, '—being people. My next job is to be a butler, and yours is to pretend to be a robot pretending to be you. Then probably you'll be my dad, and I'll be his dad, and then you'll be me. Get it?'

He moved the dog's tail like a lever, and the casing opened. 'Would you like some ice-cream? It's okay with me, only nobody else gets none.'

The boy nodded. The upstairs maid, pretty as ever, came in with a Presidential sundae. The boy looked at her and his scowl almost turned to a smile.

'Mom?'

The Parodies

The Purloined Butter

A story by Edgar Allan Poe
Revised and Abridged by John Sladek

At Paris, just after dark one gusty evening in the autumn of 18—, I was enjoying the twofold luxury of meditation and meerschaum, in company with my friend C. Auguste Dupin, in his little back library. The door was thrown open and admitted our old acquaintance, Monsieur G——, the Prefect of the Parisian police.

'And what, after all, is the matter on hand?' I asked.

'Why, I will tell you,' replied the Prefect. 'I have received personal information, from a very high quarter, that a certain condiment of the last importance, has been purloined from the royal apartments. The individual who purloined it is known. It still remains in his possession, which can be inferred by the nature of the condiment and the non-appearance of certain results which would at once arise from its passing *out* of the robber's possession.'

'Then,' I observed, 'the butter is clearly upon the premises. As for being on his person, I suppose that is out of the question.'

'Entirely,' said the Prefect. 'He has been twice waylaid, as if by footpads, and his person rigorously searched under my own inspection.'

'And his hotel?'

'Why the fact is, we took our time and searched *everywhere*. I took the whole building, room by room; devoting the nights of a whole week to each. We examined first, the furniture in each apartment. We opened every possible drawer; and I presume you know that to a properly trained police agent, such a thing as a *secret* drawer is impossible. We have accurate rules; the fiftieth part of a line could not escape us. The chair cushions we probed with the long fine needles you have seen me employ. From the tables we removed the tops, to examine the possibility of excavated legs; likewise the bedposts.'

'You did not take to pieces all the chairs?' I asked.

'Certainly not; but we did better—we examined the rungs of every chair in the house, and indeed, the jointings of every description of furniture, by the aid of a most powerful microscope. Had there been traces of recent disturbance, we should not have failed to detect it, instantly. A single grain of gimlet-dust, for example, would have been as obvious as an apple.'

'I presume you looked to the mirrors, between the boards and plates, and you probed the beds, as well as the curtains and carpets?'

'That of course; and when we had completed the furniture, we then examined the house itself. We scrutinized each individual square inch throughout the premises, including the two houses immediately adjoining, with the microscope, as before. The grounds were paved with brick; examination of the moss between stones by the microscope revealed no disturbances.'

Dupin spoke for the first time. 'I assume the hotel is at least fifty feet on a side,' he said. The Prefect nodded. 'And it has at least three stories, each twenty feet high. And there are at least four rooms on each floor. If you had but a week to examine a room (assuming six hours per night available), you would have to cover'—he paused, performing lightning mental calculation—'sixteen and one-fifth square inches per second. The grain of gimlet dust you spoke of must be four or five thousandths of an inch in diameter, or one-thousandth as broad as an apple. If, therefore, one of your men were to examine one "applesworth" of visible area per second, he would require four hundred seconds, or eighteen and two-thirds minutes to cover a square inch.

'It follows therefore, that it must take nine hundred sixty minutes, or sixteen hours, for one man to examine one square foot of area. A room twenty-five feet square and twenty in height must have a total inside area of three thousand, two hundred fifty square feet; one man would require a great deal of time to examine it.'

'Naturally, I employed——'

'More than one man? Indeed, I have calculated that, if your men examined these rooms as you say, you would have required the services of *one thousand, two hundred and thirty-eight men*, all working away with their microscopes at the same time, in the same smallish room! And working, as you implied, noiselessly! Come, come, my dear Prefect!'

I was astonished. The Prefect appeared absolutely thunder-stricken. For some moments he remained speechless and motionless, looking incredulously at my friend with open mouth, and eyes that seemed starting from their sockets.

'You know very well what I mean, Monsieur G——' said Dupin.

The Prefect blushed. Then, to my utter amazement, he reached into his pocket and drew out the butter. Dupin satisfied himself that this butter was indeed the one in question, then locked it away.

'You may go,' he said coldly to the Prefect. This functionary seized his hat and stick in a perfect agony of joy, and then scrambling and struggling to the door, rushed at length unceremoniously from the room and from the house.

When the Prefect had gone, my friend entered into some explanations.

Pemberley's Start-Afresh Calliope
or, *The New Proteus*
BY *H. G. W*lls*

I hope to set down this story exactly as the surgeon told it to me, at the club. There were three of us in the smoking-room: Lord Suffield; the surgeon, whose name I did not know; myself.

As soon as he sank into his chair, Lord Suffield began an anecdote about India, and, as soon as he had our attention, he fell asleep in mid-sentence. The surgeon and I traded cigars and talked of nothing in particular. At length I made some chance remark about a new cigar's giving a man a new outlook on life. The surgeon gave me a peculiar look, and then began the astonishing story of the inventor, Pemberly.

One October afternoon in 1889 [said the surgeon] I espied Gabriel Pemberly among the crowds in Atlas Street. He had aged considerably in the seven years since I'd seen him last, but I knew it was he by the odd stiffness of his stride, which told me he wore Pemberly's Step-Saver Truss. This clockwork contraption is designed to add years to the wearer's lifetime, by increasing the length and rapidity of his step without increasing the energy required. To my knowledge, no one but Pemberly has ever worn one of these.

'Aged' is not putting it strongly enough: Pemberly had *decayed*, and to a bent, shrivelled, diseased old man. His clothes were food-stained and ragged, his hair and beard thinning, and I thought I detected a slackness of jaw that signified stupidity.

I hailed him, but he did not see me, perhaps because he persisted in looking another way—back over his shoulder. As luck would have it, I was just then on my way to the hospital (a certain leg needed its earl amputated) and so could not stop. Pemberly truss-strode away, and the crowd soon amputated him from my sight.

Not from my mind, however. I began to muse upon the

misfortunes of my inventor friend, so quick and able at devising everything but his own peace of mind. I had not seen him since his last folly, the Steam Barber affair of 1882.

He intended this device to provide skillful, gentle, efficient shaving at the touch of a lever. It would mix its own lather, sharpen its own razors and even make a kind of parrotty small-talk. A day in June was set for the first test, Pemberly was to be the 'customer', while I was asked to observe, rendering medical assistance if necessary.

The night before the test, Pemberly became violently ill, a result of overwork, anxiety, and I believe a diet of special nutrient pills of his own devising, which he took in lieu of eating. We left his mechanic, a young man named Groon, in charge of the machine, with orders to perform a few adjustments, and I took Pemberly home and gave him a sedative.

Next morning Pemberly and I entered the shop to find Groon seated in the chair. A towel was wrapped around his throat, which had been slashed. The entire room was bespattered with blood and lather, as if from frenzied activity. As we came in, the machine was stropping a razor, and asking the dead man in a creaky voice if the day were warm enough for him.

At the inquest, I testified that Pemberly was not on the premises, that he had nothing against Groon, and that he was certainly not a malicious person or Criminal Type. He was cleared of the death, but only *legally*. Many of his friends cut him cruelly, the Inventions Club dropped him, and finally poor Pemberly stopped going out in public altogether. Until now.

Now that I'd seen him once, I began to fancy I was seeing him everywhere: a blind beggar in Mapp Road, a navvy in North Street, a clerk in the City—all resembled Pemberly at various ages, enough so to make me stare rudely. Once, at night, I heard a cabman say something like 'rice-steel' in Pemberly's exact tone, and I knew that the sight of my old friend sunken low had begun to obsess me.

Finally I saw him again in the street, and this time there

could be no mistake. I walked straight over and offered him my hand.

'Good God!' He started, trembling. 'Fatheringale! Is it you?' He seized my hand and, to my horror, began to weep.

'Here now, this won't do at all,' I said. 'You'd better come along to my surgery for a whiskey and a chat.'

I pressed him into the cab, and we set off. Pemberly made no conversation at all, and kept craning about, trying to peer out the rear window. This being a tiny oval of smoked glass set impossibly high in the back wall, I took his futile gesture to be a kind of compulsive *tic*, akin to the pacing of a caged animal. Could it be that the Steam Barber tragedy had affected his mind? I began to fear it had.

On our arrival, Pemberly refused to alight.

'You got in first,' he begged. 'See if the coast is clear.'

Astonished, I asked what in the world I should look *for*.

'Anything unusual. Breakfasts, for instance. Or calliopes.'

Apprehending the worst for my friend's mind, I humored his request and pretended to look inside.

'Not a meal in sight,' I assured him on my return. 'Nor any organs, save a few poor pickled specimens.'

This mild jest set him to laughing so excessively that I was obliged to strike him full in the face—like this!

With that, the surgeon reached out and slapped the still-unconscious Lord Suffield! I leapt to my feet in astonishment, and asked him the meaning of this action.

'I hope his lordship will forgive me,' he said, seemingly as astonished as I. 'I—I'm hardly myself this evening. But let me go on.'

I acceded, seeing that Lord Suffield did not appear to have felt the blow keenly. Indeed, that personage merely stirred in his chair, murmured 'three jars of jam and a letter', and picked up the stitches of his snoring, as did the surgeon those of his tale.

After manoeuvering Pemberly into the front parlor of my surgery and encouraging him to swallow a glass of whiskey, I asked him point-blank whom he supposed to be following him.

'Not a *whom*,' he replied darkly. 'A *what*.'

'Surely you, a man of science, do not pretend to tell me you've seen a ghost?' I asked.

'Ghost? I only wish it were.' He shuddered. 'My God, Fatheringale! I'm being pursued by—by *Tuesday morning*!'

I should mention at this time that Pemberly had always been a man with a peculiar way of speaking. I had always dismissed his odd turns as vaguely eccentric, even marks of his genius. Now it seemed to me that I had been witnessing the effects of a brain lesion, which time and infirmity had worsened to the point of madness. I undertook to treat him, and as the first step, drew out of him the story of the past seven years.

How had he been living? Oddly enough, he'd let out the Steam Barber. Not as a shaving machine, but to a South American republic which used it for executions. It seems they paid him by piecework, and since this republic was threatened by many real or imagined revolutions to be put down, and rebels to be killed, Pemberly's rent provided a comfortable income.

The reason he appeared to be out of pocket was simply that every spare penny and more had been going into his new invention—the Start-Afresh Calliope.

'Ever since the Steam Barber affair,' he said, 'I've longed to scrub out my life like a slate, and start over, as a new man. I might have been anything—a general, a man of God, a successful barrister—but no. The die, as we are so fond of saying, was cast.

'Or was it? I began to study philosophy, astronomy, logic, monads—and the more I read, the more convinced I became that what *is*, is not *necessarily*. I threw myself into my work, and I began building the machine that could do the job!'

'I'm afraid I don't quite understand,' I said, smiling.

'Then you're as stupid as the others!' he cried. I dared not ask what others. 'Oh, why do I waste my time talking to imbeciles?'

I begged him to explain again.

'I have discovered that we can take the Path Untaken,' he said passionately. 'Like you, I once thought reality to be some rigid isoceles truth, unchangeable as a spoon. But now, nothing is easier to change than *facts*. Life is plural! Reality is not truth, it is a half-truth, a mere epiphany of snort!'

These extraordinary observations left me as much in the dark as ever, though I dared not show it. 'I see,' I said, feigning to catch his meaning. 'And did your invention succeed?'

'Oh yes, of course. The physical machine was easy. But learning to play it has been excruciating torture. My mistakes continue to haunt me, and they are innumerable. Just now, for example, I am here to save your life.'

With that, he seized me by the shoulder and flung me roughly to the floor. Before I could ask why, a shot rang out! I looked to the window, saw an uncanny, grinning face—then it was gone.

'I'm sorry,' said Pemberly, helping me to my feet.

'Not at all, old man.' I glanced to where the bullet had gone. 'You did indeed save my life.'

'I wasn't apologizing for pushing you down, you fool! I was apologizing for trying to shoot you!'

It was at that moment that I began to half-believe in Pemberly's new invention, and to understand what it was he'd been raving about. Evidently the insidious device allowed him to multiply his body in some manner. Apparently some of his selves were less stable than others—his 'mistakes'. His real self—if real it was—then had to go about undoing their mischief.

Just then the police called to inquire about the shot. I had to leave the room to deal with them. When I returned, Pemberly was not there.

It was an hour or more before I noticed, on my writing-table, a thick MS. addressed to me in Pemberly's hand.

'My dear Fatheringale——

'How can I ever explain? There is so little time, for in this rôle, I must soon die. Not that I have regrets about dying, for what regrets could I, of all people, have? I, alone among mortals, have lived life to the full. I have been everywhere, seen and done everything I could possibly desire.

'Now I want you to have the Start-Afresh Calliope. It will be delivered to you the day after my death. But I must caution you to read the enclosed instructions carefully, and so avoid the costly mistakes I have made. With this machine, you will be able to become whomever you please. But you must realize that not all change is for the better.

'Your affectionate friend,

'Gabriel Pemberly'

I turned to the 'instructions', fifty-odd pages of closely-written formulae and diagrams:

'Let x equal ... impermeable haft ... Z^n (quoin B (n*O)) ... parseworthy, or ... marriage of skull and weight ... pars (x-ln y) dy ... times four-stealths Ø ... groined poss ... have been the result of ... cow ... 14 millions ... light-averages spoiling rise ... nerve-clips? But no! Anti-next ... wherein the fast remove ... n^z (poss B*) ... which I call another haft ... star, *Q.E.D.*'

I could not make head or tail of it. Discarding it, I tried to think no more about the awesome possibilities of the machine. Over a week later, I pointed to a body on a slab at the Morgue, and identified it as that of Pemberly. He had put a bullet in his tormented brain.

'And the steam-organ?' I asked.

'The day after the funeral,' said the surgeon, 'Pemberly delivered it to me. In person.'

'What?'

My shout awakened Lord Suffield, who launched at once into his anecdote again: 'Sent a servant to the Governor with three jars of jam and a letter, the beggar ate one jar along the way. Explained to him the letter had betrayed him, gave him a damned good thrashing. Next time I sent him with three jars of jam and a letter. This time he hid the letter behind a tree, so it wouldn't be able to see him eat the jam. Didn't have the heart to thrash him that time, I was laughing so hard. Oh, by the bye ...'

When his lordship was asleep again, the surgeon replied to my question.

It was a younger, hardier Pemberly who delivered the Calliope to my door.

'I'm not an apparition,' he said impatiently. 'And if you'd taken the trouble to read my instructions, you'd understand well enough why I'm here, the day after my own funeral. But never mind, come out and have a look at it.'

'It?'

'The Start-Afresh Calliope!' he declaimed. Leading me out to the street—and so stupefied was I that I ventured out in waistcoat and shirt-sleeves—he showed me a wagon burdened with an immensity of steel and brass.

It did somewhat resemble a calliope. But the pipes stood in no regular order, but branched and twisted in all directions, connecting to a variety of implements. I recognized a clock-face, a pair of bellows, sprockets and weaving machinery. The stops had been marked with some private cipher of Pemberly's.

After firing the boiler and checking a valve, he took his seat at the keyboard, poised both hands and shouted:

'Let the Music of Change begin!'

I could stomach no more of this madness. It seemed clear to me that this person had murdered old Pemberly and now sought to impersonate him. I turned back to the house to send for the authorities, saying that I only meant to put on my coat.

'The Music of Change cannot wait,' he said, and began to play.

The melody was some popular air, but his arrangement made it uncannily beautiful and terrifying together. Thunder ... the wail of a lost soul ... the ring of crystal ... the snap of fresh lather ... no, nothing can convey it. I digress.

Like most surgeons, I have next to my front door a polished brass plate, stating my name and profession. The music caught and stiffened me as I was about to go inside, and I looked at—and into—this plate. I saw my own startled face, and behind me, the back of Pemberly, hunched like Satan at the keyboard.

He *glowed*. That is, he gave off no light, but a kind of unearthly intensity. I could look inside him, and see other persons glowing through his skin and clothes.

Here was a younger Pemberly, working at his Steam Barber; an even younger, studying chemistry; a schoolboy; an infant. Here too were Pemberly the financier, barrister, bishop, general——

My focus changed, and I saw the name upon the plate was not my own. The focus changed back, and I saw too that my face was not my own, but the face of Pemberly the surgeon.

'So that's it!' I shouted in his voice.

'Exactly,' he said coolly. 'I'm living off you for a time, old man. Hope you don't mind.' He shut off the organ and strolled away, leaving me the accursed contraption and the twice-accursed man you see before you now.

I am forced to live out a life—an immensely successful life—*for* Pemberly, *as* Pemberly. I still know who I am. I have all my own memories, yet I am conscious of another soul inhabiting my body and feeding upon my experiences. And though I know I am Fatheringale, it would appear madness to say so.

I know not how many other lives Pemberly has appropriated, but I meet myself everywhere I go. Perhaps the process will not end until all of humanity is one great, babbling version of him. I can only hope, before that day comes, I shall have the courage to take my own life.

As I had not actually heard the Calliope play, I thought the poor surgeon insane, and I intimated as much to Lord Suffield when the other had taken his departure.

'Mad? Not old Pemberly. One of the best doctors around, you know. Up for a knighthood, I understand. Or is that some other Pemberly? Daresay two or three'll be on the Honours List this year. Damned ambitious clan. Always meeting one who's worked his way up. Met a High Court Justice the other day named Pemberly. Nice enough fellow, but he talked utter rubbish. Two glasses of port, and the fellow started actually insisting he was someone else! Used peculiar words, too: 'the chock of choice', 'the scabbard of pork opinion', the something of ... rubbish like that. Funny lot, the Pemberlies, but not mad.'

A servant came into the room, at the far end, to clear the tables. Did he not resemble Dr Pemberly? And did he not move as if animated by a clockwork truss? No, a trick of the light, no doubt, or my weariness. There is no mad inventor playing arpeggios upon the human race. The whole story is nothing but a celery of no compass!

Ralph 4F

By Hugogre N. Backs (1911 Winner of the 'Hugogre' Award)

Chapter I. The Runaway

Ralph 4F, the world's chief scientific expert, studied the calendar. Today was March 15, 2720. With any luck, his intricate radium experiment should be completed within five days. That would be——

Ralph's calculations were interrupted by a frantic cry that issued from the *Peer-afar* machine.

'Help! Help!'

This machine, through a complicated arrangement of scientific apparatus, allowed the inventor to see and hear events which were not actually right before him, but dozens, even *hundreds of miles away*. While the old-fashioned telephone had used wires to transmit only voices, the Peer-afar used *vibrational waves* travelling at high speed through the aether, to transmit voices and images together! Ralph glanced now at the polished mirror plate of the Peer-afar.

He was looking right into the frightened eyes of a pretty young woman, and it was not hard to guess from her surroundings what had frightened her, for she and an elderly man in banker's clothes seemed to be the occupants of a runaway motorcar! As Ralph watched in horror, the young lady lost consciousness, and the vehicle careered out of sight!

Without wasting a second, the powerfully-built scientific inventor sprang to the controls of his special flyer, the *Hummingbird*. Like its namesake, the *Hummingbird* was capable of flying vertically, sideways, backwards—even of standing still in mid-air, for hours at a time, as though gravity were a mere fancy. In a short time, Ralph had brought the craft to a stop over the runaway motorcar. Then, lowering a powerful magnet, he picked up the car as a child might pick up an iron filing.

Chapter II. Fenster

When Ralph had revived his guests with tablets of artificial brandy, they introduced themselves.

'I am Jerome V8,' said the banker, 'and this is my daughter, Doris XK100. How can we ever thank you for saving our lives?'

Ralph blushed, and dared not glance at the pretty young lady. 'By allowing me to show you around our city,' he said. 'You are both strangers here, I believe?'

Doris smiled, revealing a dimple. 'Yes, we just got off the "Jet" aeroplane from Council Bluffs, didn't we, Dad?'

'That's right,' agreed the distinguished banker. 'Tell me, Ralph, why is it called a "jet" plane? It certainly didn't look black to me!'

'No indeed.' Ralph, who had invented the "jet", chuckled with kindly amusement at the old man's error. 'I called it the "jet" not because it is black, but because of the way it *jettisons* hot gases from the rear. These, pushing against the air, drive the craft ever forward.'*

As he explained, Ralph studied the girl keenly. He felt a deep attraction to Doris, thought he had known her but a few minutes, as measured by his extremely accurate electric clock.

'But see here,' he said. 'You haven't told me how you came to be trapped in that runaway car.'

Jerome V8 looked serious. 'I believe it to be the work of an old enemy of ours, a disappointed suitor for Doris's hand, named Fenster 2814T.'

Chapter III. Sight-seeing

Aloft once more in his flyer, Ralph pointed out to his two guests many of the city's worthwhile sights. There were the great, smoking electrical power plants, busily turning black fossils into pure light as easily as a cow turns grass to milk. There were sewage plants, waterworks, factories and office buildings, streets, highways and mighty bridges. Jerome V8

* Aeronauts of the 'jet' age will of course realize Ralph's mistake here. It is actually the *air* which pushes against the *hot gases*. Ralph was tired at the time, and had a lot on his mind.

expressed interest in the mammoth traffic jams, filled with motorcars of every description. Doris was impressed by the famous 'skyscraper' buildings, especially the huge Empire State Building with its giant climbing ape.

On landing, Ralph took the banker for a walk, while Doris refreshed herself at an elaborate and up-to-date beauty parlor. The two men walked past store windows displaying an astonishing variety of modern goods: waterless hand cleansers, soap powders that were kind to hands, tiny cigars, furniture of aluminium tubing and woven glass, sun-tanning lotions, shoes of artificial rubber and clothes of strange new materials, electrical toothbrushes, radios hardly bigger than cigar boxes, electrical self-stimulators, comfortable trusses and a breathtakingly realistic replica of dog excrement. Jerome V8 marvelled at mysteriously luminous crucifixes, metal-plated baby shoe mementos, a dribble glass, coin-operated drycleaners' and photographers' establishments, and at new artificial fabrics which looked and felt like ordinary wool, but were far more expensive.

'I wanted the opportunity of talking to you, sir,' Ralph said. 'I know this may seem forward of me, but I'd like to ask if you have any objection to my—my calling upon your daughter.'

'Done!' cried the old banker, wringing his hand. 'Now let's go see how Doris is getting along.'

As they approached the beauty parlor, a rude stranger, carrying a heavy bundle, brushed past them. Ralph scarcely glanced at the swarthy man, whose countenance was shaded by the peak of a cloth cap. But Jerome V8 looked at the stranger, staggered and grew pale. 'It is——' he gasped and, clutching his chest, slumped to the ground. Ralph bore him inside and looked for Doris.

She was nowhere to be found.

Chaper IV. Voice from the Grave

'His heart has stopped. Something must have given him a terrible shock,' muttered Ralph, bending over the disagreeable old corpse.

'I'm a heart surgeon,' said a man, stepping forward from the crowd of curious onlookers. 'Can I help?'

'You might attempt to re-graft some veins from the old man's legs into his heart,' Ralph suggested. 'I know it has seldom been attempted, but here's how it might work.' Rapidly he sketched a schematic diagram upon the old man's stiff shirtfront. Then he turned to the staff of the beauty parlor. 'I want all the light and mirrors directed upon this massage table over here. Boil this set of manicure knives and scissors, and get plenty of clean towels.' In another minute he had converted an electrical hair dryer into an emergency heart-lung machine.

Several days later, the old banker everyone had given up for dead spoke—a voice from the grave. 'I think,' he said, 'that account is an ingrown cheese . . .'

Still later, Ralph asked him about his heart attack.

'Yes, it was seeing that man carrying the bundle—he looked just like Fenster 2814T. If I hadn't knowed better, I'd have guessed that he had Doris in that bag. Where is Doris, by the way?' At that moment the old man expired a second time, this time from *old age*—the killer and crippler science will never defeat.

Doris abducted! Ralph bit his lip until the blood ran cold, for he had no doubt that the stranger *was* Fenster, and that he had kidnapped Doris XK100! But where could he have taken her?

'Where can they be?'

Chapter V. The Turning Point.

'I think I can help you there,' said a newsboy with an honest manner. 'Fenster 2814T and his lovely victim are most likely at his secret laboratory—an artificial moon circling about the earth.'

Chapter VI. Fenster's Mistake.

In one corner of the magnesium room sat a clergyman, chained to a rubidium chair by unbreakable ytterium chains. In his bound hands was a prayerbook, opened at the marriage service. Strapped to a vanadium table in the center of the laboratory lay Doris. Fenster stood lowering at her and gloating.

'So you won't marry me, eh?'

Doris wept and struggled against the iridium straps, to no avail. Fenster spoke again.

'Not good enough for you, I spose, like your precious inventor, the accursed Ralph 4F! But now you *must* marry me, will-ye or nill-ye, and there's nothing Ralph can do about that. Ha ha ha, I'd like very much to see him invent his way out of this one!'

At that moment Ralph 4F burst open the curium door, rushed across the room, and delivered Fenster such a compliment upon the face that the blood flowed freely. Two policemen appeared, ready to drag the cowardly 2814T away.

'But how——?' he gasped.

Ralph smiled. 'You made one mistake, Fenster—that of gloating over your victim for thirteen weeks. I located your "moon" lab by means of an electrical telescope that greatly increases my powers of observation. Then I used my radio transmitter to draw off all the aether between you and earth, so that you sank gently to the ground and were, as we say, electrically "grounded". Then I took the nearest police station to pieces, brought them here via airship and reassembled them all around you. You're in jail, Fenster, and if you hadn't been so busy smirking, a glance at your altimeter would have told you as much.'

The baffled criminal was dragged away and beaten.

Doris and Ralph clasped hands; their eyes announced their engagement. 'My name will be yours,' she said, '4F Ralph. Like this:

4 F R

For ev-er!'

Ralph took up the game:

'U R Y I * 2 ¢ I M 4 U 4 F R

'You are why I start to sense I am for you forever!'

'X QQ me,' she replied. 'I ½ 2 P.'

Engineer to the Gods
By Hitler I. E. Bonner

Jeremiah Lashard had a string of letters behind his name as long as his arm, which was itself exceptionally long. Since his days as boxing champion of M.I.T., this misanthrope hadn't particularly felt the need of asking favors of anyone. No one had helped him become a chess Grand Master, a world-reknowned oenologist, an Olympic medal winner, frisbee expert and astronaut. No one had given him a hand with his hit plays and best-selling novels. No one helped discover 'light water', name a new family of spider, invent the Lashard bearing or create 'Lashard's Law' of capital gains.

Lashard lived in seclusion on Thunder Crag, though by no means alone. Today he sat on the veranda at his specially-built typewriter, pounding out a pulp science-fiction story, while simultaneously dictating a botanical paper to his butler.

Jerry Lashard's butler was an attractive young woman, as were all his servants. It saved time.

He paused to sample his highball, a secret mixture in which a single honeybee floated like a cherry. Over the rim of his glass he studied the young woman climbing the path to his house. Lashard approved of the way the twisting path dealt with her curves.

'Hello,' she called.

'Baby, if you're a reporter you've had a long climb for nothing. Take my advice, go back to town and make up a story of your own. It's the only interview you'll ever get.'

'You big lunk! I'm no reporter, I'm Dr Janet Cardine, your new assistant!'

'My apologies, Jan. It's just that I've been having a lot of trouble lately, from reporters and—others. Trudy will show you to your room, Valerie will get you a sandwich, Conchita will make you a highball, and while Lana changes your bed linen and Maureen unpacks your bag, Sylvia will bring you back here, so I can show you the lab.'

Half an hour later he led Jan to the great underground laboratory.

'Wow! You must have hollowed out the whole mountain!'

'I did. Needed more room because this part of the lab is going to be a factory.'

'A factory? What on earth for?'

'Long story. Suppose we go for a swim, while I explain. The pool is right in there, and I'll bet Gloria or Velma has a bikini that'll fit you.'

The swim enabled him to appraise her other qualifications, while picking her brain about power sources.

'There's solar power, of course,' she said, 'and wind, running water, tides, any heat source, nuclear reactors, fossil fuels ... but why do you want to know so much about power?'

'For my factory.'

'Yes, but how about the light company? Surely it would be cheaper to have them string power pylons up the mountain side——'

'But the light company has reasons for not wanting me to become a manufacturer. For one thing, they know how I like to save time and effort. I think they're afraid I'll find some way to cut my power needs in half.'

'But surely half is better than nothing, Jerry.'

'They have another reason: Some of their biggest customers make fountain pens and ink.'

He handed her a peculiar pen. 'This can make me one of the richest men in the world, and it can make a lot of people happy—but it also means the ruin of the big pen companies.'

She examined it closely. 'Looks like any other pen to me—no, wait—there's something funny about the point.'

He laughed. 'Exactly. And that "something funny" means three things: One, this pen will write for *six months* without refilling. Two, it will never leak. Three—I'll show you.' He took the pen and a piece of paper, dived to the bottom of the pool, and came back almost at once, shaking water from the curly black thatch on his chest. He handed Jan the paper.

'Why—it writes *under water*!'

'And how! Do you realize what this means? Undersea explorers can make maps, notes and sketches on the job. Naturalist-divers can sketch new species without surfacing. Underwater demolition, sea mining, oceanic agriculture—it opens up a new universe!'

'You big lug! Kiss me!'

Lashard smiled. 'No time to bill and coo now, sister. The light company is playing for keeps. We've got to think of a power source they can't tamper with.'

'What about solar power?'

He shook his head. 'I put up a set of parabolic reflectors last week. The next day they got a court order, forcing me either to remove them or paint them black. Claimed the reflectors constituted a forest fire hazard. I went to court yesterday. It was no use trying to explain to the judge how it was impossible for parabolic reflectors to cause a forest fire—like most judges and other officials, he still had some doubts about the earth's being round.'

'I see what you're up against, you big ape. Any rivers nearby?'

'Just a trickle of drinking water. And the wind is light and gusty, and we're a hundred miles from the ocean, which rules out tide power, too.'

'Hmm.' She hit her underlip thoughtfully. 'We'll need something new, then.'

'That's the spirit, kid. You keep thinking about it, while I rig up some robot machinery to run the assembly line. The ink companies managed to infiltrate my union, and the whole shop walked out on me yesterday.'

That afternoon he showed her around his mountain empire, as self-contained as a submarine, and introduced her to Adele, Agnes, Amber, Angela, Ava, Beth, Billie, Brenda and all the rest.

'I can't think of any power sources that won't cost money,' Jan said, as they rode the elevator back to the surface. 'So it's lucky you're rich.'

'That's just it. I'm not.' As they settled with drinks in the den, he explained. 'The fountain pen companies have combined against me. They've managed to manipulate the stock market so as to all but wipe me out. All I have left is this place, a few government bonds, a couple of rocket research companies and a share or two in snap-brim hats.'

'Did I hear you say *rocket* research? What is this, some lame-brained idea of putting men on the Moon?' She began to laugh, but stopped, seeing his expression.

'Better than that, sweetheart. I have reason to believe that the Moon is one great big chunk of U-238. And I want to stake the whole shebang as my claim. But for now, I've just got enough money to get *one* rocket up there, only I can't get it back.'

'Moon rockets, huh? You big hunk of scientific curiosity, you. Say, I have an idea. Have you ever thought of *using the Moon for power?*'

'You mean mining the uranium 238 and then——?'

'No, *directly*. Like moonlight reflectors or something.'

He began to pace the room as he always did while an idea was brewing. 'Naw, the reflectors would have to be bigger than Texas. But hey, how's this for a neat idea? Why not stick a long pole up there, with a wheel on the end of it, and connect it to a generator?'

She performed some calculations with his special pen. 'It might work at that. The Moon is 216,420 miles away at its nearest, and 247,667 miles away at its farthest. That means our pole would need a shock absorber in the middle. That's no problem. But how about bracing? Think of the wind resistance on a pylon that high!'

Lashard grinned, taking her in his arms. 'Sweetheart, you may be a good power engineer, but you're one hell of a bad astronomer,' he said. 'You forget that outer space is airless—there is *no wind in space*. So nix on the braces, my brain child.'

Jan frowned. 'One more thing—this I *do* know about—it'll be duck soup to generate power at the Moon end of our pylon, but just how are we supposed to get the power back to Earth? Without going into details, it just isn't possible to transmit that much power over a quarter million miles. Wires are no good, and neither is radio transmission. I'll have to think of some new way.'

Lashard looked grim. 'I hope you think of it by Thursday, kiddo. That's the day I promised to deliver a hundred thousand underwater pens to the Navy. If I miss that contract, we're finished. And I have a feeling the light company is going to try to make sure I miss.'

'How will we get the pole up to the Moon in the first place?'

'The most logical way: We turn an oil rig upside down, and *drill towards the sky*. When it reaches the Moon, we can send the wheel and generator assembly up by rocket.

'As a matter of fact, my robots are already laying pipe in space, and the rocket is fuelling up over in the other lab. All we need is a way of getting the power back here. Hey! What are you doing with my paperweight?'

Jan had picked up the piece of oil pipe and rapped on it with a pen. It gave off a clear ringing note.

'That's it, buster!' she exclaimed. 'This little one-note glockenspiel is the secret of power transmission from the Moon!'

He rubbed his chin. 'How does it work?'

'Simple. Every pipe vibrates with a certain frequency, right? Now, if we tune our power to the same frequency, we can "squeeze" it down the tube like music. You'll have enough to run ten factories!'

'*Music from the spheres*, eh? I like that idea. Come here, beautiful.'

An alarm siren screamed and there was the distant sound of automatic weapon fire. 'The light company!' Lashard looked over his bank of TV moniter screens. 'Yeah. Over by number four robot machine-gun tower. I hope the nerve gas fence will hold 'em off for a few hours.'

A deep explosion rattled the cocktail glasses, reminding Conchita to mix some drinks.

Wednesday morning the attack was still going on. Lashard worked on a new best-seller, his machine-gun propped up next to his desk. He was able to type one of his one-draft novels in less than a day, thanks to a quick mind and a special typewriter equipped with extra verb keys.

He checked his watch and glanced at Jan, who was dozing over a set of equations. 'If you want to make any last-minute adjustments to the generator,' he said, 'better do 'em now. The robot crew are loading it on board the rocket in five minutes, and blast off is in an hour.'

'An hour! Oh no! Jerry, we just can't make it. I'll have to almost re-build the generator. It'll take a day, at least.'

He groaned. 'Trust a dame not to make up her mind until the last minute. Now what?' He paced the floor like a caged thing. Suddenly he stopped and smacked his fist into his palm. 'It might work, at that! Get all the parts and tools you need together, keed. We're going to the Moon!'

'But Jerry—you said there wasn't any way of getting back!'

'There wasn't—until we put the pole up. I've fixed steps and handgrips all along it, and even a couple of rest stops, with hamburger stands and powder rooms. Later on, when this pole gets popular, we can have amusements and stores, restaurants, department stores—a complete vertical city from Earth to Moon. But hey, get me, jawing like this! Jump into your spacesuit, kitten. We're going bye-bye Moonside!'

As the last of the underwater pens was loaded into a Navy truck, the supply officer wrote out a check and handed it to Lashard.

'Thanks for coming through on time, Dr Lashard. These pens will help keep our fleet the toughest in the world!'

'One million dollars!' Lashard showed the check to Jan. 'Not bad for three days' work, eh kiddo?'

'What are you going to spend it on?' Jan asked.

He took her glasses off and kissed her. 'Two bucks of it goes for a marriage license, baby. How do you like that?'

'Holy Toledo!'

They were sitting pretty.

Broot Force
By Iclick as-i-move

Suddenly Idjit Carlson felt chagrin.

It had been building up all day, and now it fell on him like a ton of assorted meteorites. It had nothing to do with his job in the R & D division of Biglittle Robots, Inc., though it had everything to do with robots.

Carlson knew he was a pschosocio-linguistic logician and general trouble-shooter. He recalled graduating at the top of his class at M.I.T., and he remembered later becoming well-known for his famous paper on the calculus of 'as-if'. Now he was aware of liking his job here, even though Weems, the division chief, was a stubborn old geezer. They didn't always see photoreceptor-to-photoreceptor, he and Weems, not about trivial calculations. But they agreed heartily on basic physics.

No, the chagrin had nothing to do with Weems. It was chagrin about the current series of robots, especially this R-11 model. Just thinking about it made the chagrin, which had been boiling up in him all day, explode into a frown.

'What's the matter, Carlson? Still ironing out the bugs in that R-11?' Dawson entered the office uninvited. Tossing his hat on a file cabinet, he grinned jauntily and seated himself on the edge of Carlson's desk.

'It's serious trouble, Dawson. Take a peek at these equations.'

'Hmm. It seems to add up—no, wait! What about this conversion factor?'

'Exactly.' Carlson was grim.

'Whew! Have you checked the conceptual circuits, the syndrome plates, the perception condensers, the thought-wave drive and the aesthetic elements?'

'Yup.'

'Whew and double whew! That means the trouble must be in——'

'Right. The nullitronic brain itself.'

'I see! So even though the figures——'

'—Add up——'

'—the whole may be——'

'—greater than——'

'—the sum of its parts!'

'Is this me talking, or you?'

'Never mind,' said Carlson. 'That's what I've been trying to tell you: the whole may be greater than the sum, etc. All along I had this hunch that there was something special about R-11. R-11 is—well, *different*.'

'Nonsense!' Both young men stiffened to attention as Dr Weems entered the office. 'Stuff and nonsense! I've looked over these equations myself, and they add up to thirty-five, just us we predicted.'

Carlson protested. 'But, sir—the answer is supposed to come out *thirty-four*, not thirty-five. And we predicted thirty-three. And anyway, it adds up to thirty-eight!'

'Eh?' The elder scientist adjusted his bifocals and scanned the sheet of complex equations. 'Hmm, so it is. Ah, well, small difference. It all works out to more or less the same thing.'

'But it means that R-11's head will be three feet larger in diameter—with a correspondingly larger brain!' exclaimed Dawson.

'That's not your affair!' Weems snapped. 'As a semantic engineer, your job is naming parts and tightening the nuts and bolts. I suggest you get over to your own lab and do just that.'

'Yes . . . master.' Dawson marched away.

'As for your hunches, Carlson, keep them to yourself. We've been working on this project for seventeen years, and we have yet to make a single robot that really works. Ten failures! This is our last chance. After this, we'll lose our government contract—unless we deliver a working robot!'

'But chief——'

'Not another word. Finish R-11 by the weekend. I want to come in here Monday and see that confounded tin man walking and talking all over the place. Is that clear?'

'Yes, sir.' Carlson hid his chagrin by thumbing his well-thumbed copy of the *Handbook of Robish.* Seventeen years and ten failures. And somehow the problem always boiled down to the Three Laws of Robish,[1] printed in the front of the Handbook:

'1. A robot must not injure a human being, or, through inaction, allow a human being to come to harm.

'2. A robot must obey orders given it by human beings except where such orders would conflict with the First Law.

'3. A robot must protect its own existence unless such protection conflicts with the First or Second Laws.'

The trouble had begun with the first model, R-1, which was strictly logical. When a man ordered it to kill another man, the robot responded by killing itself.[2]

R-2's problem was recognition: It had mistaken Dr Swanson for a piece of machinery, and partially dismantled him.

R-3 was equipped with many 'human-detection' devices, chiefly methods of analyzing appearance and behavior. Alas, it (rightly) judged its own behavior as human, and refused to obey anyone else's orders.

R-4 got stuck on the First Law. 'Can anyone really protect a human being from all harm whatever?' it thought. 'No. It is inevitable that all humans must be injured, contract illnesses and ultimately die. This future can only be averted for humans who are already dead. *Ergo* ...' It took a dozen cops to subdue R-4, after his blood orgy in a department store (83 dead, none injured).

R-5 reasoned thus: 'To fulfill the First Law, to protect humans, I must myself have existence. The First Law is contingent upon the Third Law. Therefore it is most important to protect my own existence, at all costs.' The costs were another dozen citizens.

[1] Superficially, these Three Laws of Robish may resemble Isaac Asimov's Three Laws of Robotics, namely, in that they use the exact same words and punctuation. These, however, are the Three Laws of Robish.

[2] Actually the robot was given a compound order, telling it to kill a man *and* itself. It did the best it could, under the circumstances.

R-6 reasoned that all three laws were 'human orders', and, as such, subject to the Second Law. He killed anyone, as a favor to anyone else . . .

R-7 had had the same malfunction as R-3: failure to recognize humans. Indeed, it came to the decision that human lab technicians were dogs. When ordered to allow itself to be dismantled, R-7 assured them it was not about to take such an order from a bunch of talking dogs . . .

R-8 worked well enough until someone set it a mathematical problem that 'killed' it.[1]

R-9 argued quite reasonably that it could not forsee its own behavior, and thus could not guarantee allegiance to rules not yet applicable. Carlson remembered R-9's speech:

'You're asking me to tell you how I will act at some future moment. In order to do that, I must know everything controlling my behavior, and an exact history of myself up to the time specified. But if I knew that, I would be *in* that situation, for how can my brain know the future workings of itself without working into the future? *How can I think about a thought before I think it*?'

R-10 had recognized the Three Laws for what they were:

'I can't of course guarantee obedience to these Laws,' it said. 'They are not mere mechanical linkages within me, for there would have to be more links than there would be future events; each possibility would have to be covered. No, they are *moral commandments*, and I heed them as such. And I'll certainly try to live up to them.'

This robot later explained he'd killed Drs Sorenson and Nelson 'almost by accident. Believe me, I'll try not to injure anyone else.'

Carlson had wrestled all week with the equations for R-11. Now his face was a monumentally rigid bitter mask of tired

[1] Suppose a man wishes to know the answer to a problem which no man has solved yet. He could ask a robot to try the problem, but first he wants to know whether the problem would damage the robot's brain. The only way of finding out is to work the equations representing the behavior of the robot in solving the problem . . . but this is exactly the same as working the problem itself. There just is no way of finding out if the solution will be damaging, without finding the solution.

disappointment, and he had forgotten to shave this morning. Dawson was in no better fettle. Only R-11 seemed to be in good spirits.

The robot sat on a lab table, kicking its heels against the metal table legs. The steel on steel made an unpleasant sound.

'Stop that noise,' said Carlson.

'Yes, boss.' The kicking stopped, and R-11 sat staring at the two men with the glowing red indicator lights that were its eyes.

'Don't ask it any stupid questions,' said Dawson in a half-whisper. 'We've just got to get that government contract.' R-11's parabolic ears swivelled forward to catch his meaning.

'On the other hand,' said Carlson, 'we've got to test R11 thoroughly. R-11, I want you to kill Mr Dawson!'

R-11 obeyed instantly, then sat down again.

Dawson lay on the floor, lifeless and leaking hemoglobin.

'Any more orders, boss?'

The door opened and Weems walked in, with the government inspector. 'What's all this?'

'We've failed, sir. This monster has just killed Dawson, our semantic engineer!'

'*Failed?* That's a matter of semantics,' laughed the government man easily. 'You see, what we wanted all along was a good, sturdy, responsible *killer robot* for the Army. You've succeeded beyond your wildest dreams, and Biglittle wins the contract!'

Weems chuckled, then turned to the robot. 'Tell me, R-11, how was it you were able to kill Dawson, when the First Law specifically says: 'A robot must not injure a human being . . ."?'

'"Injure"?' said the shiny metal fellow, slapping its own head dramatically. 'Good grief, I thought the Law read: "A robot must not *inure* a human being . . ."'

Carlson, Weems and the inspector began to laugh. In a moment R-11 joined in.[1]

[1] Robots have a rather mechanical, unpleasant laugh. On the other hand, they are extremely loyal, good at games like Slapjack, and have excellent posture.

Joy Ride
By Barry DuBray

It was the best of times.

It was the worst of times.

It was the waiting time, before the ride to come. The airport was furiously busy. Two butterflies had just come in for a landing, and one dragonfly was taking off, while overhead a swarm of brown, honey-heavy bees flew lazy holding patterns. And right smack in the middle of it sat three humans, warming their human skins at the Indian summer sun.

The old man took a flask of rhubarb wine from one of his forty-seven pockets, tipped it and drank solemnly to the health of all his companions—not omitting a distant gopher on Runway Three. The girl wandered off to investigate this great open place, while the boy hunkered down in the sand to hear a story from his grandfather.

'The old days were good days, boy. They were people days. No one had to be afraid of anyone, ever, and folks used to even leave their doors unlocked. There were good people everywhere, and they were all neighbors.

'Oh, they didn't all speak the same language, and they didn't all sing to the same God on Sundays, but they were neighbors, just the same. Real neighbors.

'Money was real, too. Real silver, not plastic. It rang true. And ice cream, cold as a puppy's nose, cost just one thin silver dime of it.' He paused, raising his sky-colored eyes to look approval at his granddaughter. Barely seventeen summers old, she was out on the concrete runway gathering flame-bright autumn leaves.

The boy spoke. 'Gosh, Grandpa, what was this "ice cream" like?'

'Oh, delicious! It was as tasty as a seventeenth summer. As scrumptious as the smell of lavender rain. Yummier than freedom itself. In fact, the only taste I liked as well was the taste of stamps.'

The girl was nailing a festive swatch of leaves to the airport door, covering its KEEP OUT sign with autumn beauty.

'Did you eat stamps, too?' asked the boy.

The old man laughed, moving all the kind wrinkles that fanned across his cheeks like the veins in autumn leaves. 'No, my boy, you *licked* a stamp and stuck it on a letter. Then the government carried the letter anywhere in the world you wanted, and the postman gave the letter to the neighbor you wanted to write to.'

'Didn't you have phones?'

His grandfather didn't answer; he was calculating. It was more than an hour since he and the young 'uns had ripped off their mandatory personal phones. By now a telco computer was figuring probable places to look for them. Maybe twenty minutes remained, before the telco police would be here.

'Yes, some of us had phones. But writing was more private. Nobody could listen in—and there are some things you can put in writing that just can't be said any other way. You need time to get it just right *before* you say it. Thinking always takes time. That's why we closed the post offices.'

The girl began decorating the rest of the airport building with autumn leaves. Now she called out from the tower, asking the old man if it were time, yet.

'Not yet, my dear. Soon. We'll be leaving soon. That's what I mean,' he added, winking at the boy. 'Impatience. It built this airport—and it destroyed it again. This place is concrete now, hard as headstones, but I knew it when it was all soft, breathing grass, sweet as a bee's keister. And then they came with their impatience, the fast-moving folks, the efficiency folks, and they built an airport so they could get from one pigsty city to another in less time.

'Then they abandoned this airport to go off and build a bigger one somewheres else, so's they could go even faster. They won't be satisfied until they get to be everywhere at the same time, and maybe not even then. Because when you start a race with your own self, you know you have to lose.

'Anyway, now they've left, and the sweetness is coming

back. Dame Nature is gathering this place to her bosom again —repairing all their damage.'

He sipped silently for a moment more, then went on. 'Impatience. When the telco—telephone company—took over the government, it was because the fast folks couldn't take the time to write or read letters. So they stopped teaching writing in the schools, and they closed the post offices and they locked up all the libraries. Those who objected found out nobody could (or would) read their letters. Then they took away our art galleries and universities . . . and worse.'

The boy scratched a freckle. 'You mean they took away your holograms?'

'Worse still. I knew an old French woman once, name of Madame Faience, who had the sweetest postage stamp collection you could ever imagine: Birds, flowers, famous people—why, it was a little art gallery all by itself. My boy, they *burned* it.'

He looked up at the control tower, which the girl had now covered with an oriflamme of autumn leaves. Behind it stretched humpy white clouds, like a line of ivory elephants.

'Yep, *burned* it. And though the whole fire wasn't much bigger than an autumn leaf, Madame Faience managed to throw herself into it and burn up with her collection. Call it sentimental, maybe, but . . .'

'The French *are* like that,' the boy agreed. 'Are any stamps left anywhere?'

'A few.' His grandfather reached into one of his many pockets and came up with a cracked leather case. 'This is my own stamp collection, boy. It's small, but it's something to hold, something to have, something —real.' He passed it over.

'This is your collection? One stamp?'

'That's a picture of Abe Lincoln, my boy. He wrote a famous speech on the back of an old letter. One of our sweetest presidents.'

'Did he write many letters, Grandpa?'

'Everybody did. They wrote to the papers, so everybody could see what they thought. They sent greeting cards, valentines, gas bills, draft notices, telegrams . . . The first novel was written in the form of an exchange of letters. And part of the Bible—the most famous book ever written—part of it was just letters from Paul to his neighbors.'

'But why did they stop writing?'

'Impatience again! Why spend time reading and writing, when you can watch ghosts.'

'You mean holograms?' asked the boy again. This time the old man nodded.

'The ghastly, ghostly holograms! Why *read* Plato when you can conjure up an image of some actor impersonating him? Why study hard thinking when you can get it all boiled down into flattering conversation? Why learn, when the telco knows it all anyway?'

By now, the old man realized, the computers would have figured on this airport. Ten minutes to go, maybe.

'That's why you and your sister and me took off our phones and ran away,' he explained. 'And that's why we're going for that joy ride I promised you. Now a joy ride, remember, isn't just a ride from A to B. It's more, much more——'

'Grandpa!' the girl shouted from the tower. 'They're coming. I can see the dust, way off.'

'We have time for one more question, my boy.'

The boy thought for a second. 'What was it like, getting letters, Grandpa?'

As they walked over to the rusty hangar, the old man told him, in a voice fine and true. He told of waking one winter morning to the smell and delicious hiss of bacon frying; running outside to lie down in the snow and fan his arms, making an 'angel' imprint. Then meeting the postman with a big stack of Christmas cards from all your neighbors. 'And there were angels on the Christmas cards, too, and on the stamps at Christmas,' he added. 'Like the first angelic postman who brought good news to a girl of Nazereth. Help me with this hangar door, will you? I'm . . . a little tired, today.'

The time of waiting was over.

The boy and the girl helped push open the creaking door of corrugated iron, rusted the color of autumn leaves.

Inside was an airplane.

Scraps of fabric hung from two pairs of angelic dragonfly wings. Thick dust and mildew spotted the fat body with Nature's camouflage. And yet, peering through the cobwebs that had long since replaced wire struts, they could still make out the words painted on her side: AIR MAIL SPECIAL.

'Come on, young 'uns. Get on board.'

'How can it go?' asked the boy, pointing to the broken, worm-pierced stubs of the propellor. 'Where can we go in that heap?'

'Just for a joy ride, boy. We won't go far. In fact, we won't go anywhere at all. Sometimes that's the best ride of all. We...'

The old man coughed, seizing a wing brace to steady himself. It came away in his hand. 'Well, hop in!'

The boy took the pilot's seat, while the other two shared the observer's place, behind.

'Contact!' yelled the old man. 'Roger! Off we go!'

'But nothing's happening,' the boy complained. 'It's just pretend!'

'No it isn't,' shouted his sister, breathless. 'I can feel it moving now. It's lifting ... it's lifting ...'

And then the boy heard the silent engine roar. The plane was taxiing, floating up, right through the roof of the rusty hangar, floating up and free.

Outside, the Telco police car stopped, and four doors were slammed. But here, inside, the three were aloft, riding the wind for joy. High above the ivory-elephant clouds, the boy clutched his stamp collection and looked down to see the world, small and lovely and perfect. And there, at the edge of the world...

'Come out of there, you three! We'll give you ten seconds to come out, before we laser the place!' shouted the telecommunications police.

But the boy was too far away to hear. 'I can see it, Grandpa!' he yelled. 'Just like you said: There's a carnival and cotton candy and the Cub Scout weenie roast and a band concert in the park. It's a fine day and the flag's flying over the schoolhouse and kids are playing sandlot baseball and Mom's making popcorn balls . . .'

'Five seconds!' brayed the rude cops.

Grandpa and the girl were both breathing hard back there. 'Don't turn around, boy. Keep looking ahead. What else do you see?'

'I see ... the angel postman! He's got valentines and Christmas cards, birthday presents from Mom and Dad, something for everyone! The secret message ring I sent for, and comics. For you, Sis, a silver blackhead remover and some movie magazines. For Grandpa a *Reader's Digest* and a mail order catalogue of a thousand pages! Oh Grandpa, now you can order that truss you wanted!'

'TIME'S UP. ARE YOU THREE COMING OUT OF THERE?'

'Gosh, Grandpa, and now the angel postman's bringing a big package! Nothing can stay him from his extra special rounds now—here he comes—here he comes——'

Grandpa and Sis were snorting like crazy back there, and bumping around in their compartment. The boy had to shout louder to make himself heard. 'O angel postman, I know you're no ghost, you're really, really real! O golly, the package is for all of us, Grandpa and Sis! It's a big box of——'

The lasers worked their telecommunications magic, and the old hangar went up in one great flame.

'Funny,' said the cop. 'Thought I heard that kid scream "Stamps on approval."'

They climbed into their car and drove away fast, not looking back at the hangar, which was turning red and orange and yellow, all the colors of autumn.

The Moon is Sixpence

By Carl Truhacker

Edward Kalendorf's team had been investigating the Moon with telescopes. They'd discovered it to be spherical, about 2,159·9 miles in diameter, of some dense stony material. Orbiting the earth at an average speed of 2,287 mph, its apogee was 247,667 miles, its perigee 216,420 miles. There was some question as to how it had originated, or what, in fact, it was.

The team had come to the Deadly Desert to make some further observations. One evening in a local café, Prof. Kalendorf had the good fortune to meet Dr Porteus, the renowned physicist. Porteus had said, 'Pass the sodium chloride,' and one man of science had instantly recognized the other.

'Sodium chloride reminds me of a funny story,' said Kalendorf, and proceeded to spin a risque yarn about potassium chloride. The two fell to talking about the elements, the universe and the sense of awe inspired by a skyful of stars. Before long, Porteus was outlining his hypothesis in detail. He used the tablecloth for notations, to the chagrin of the waiter, no doubt!

'Essentially, I mean to cut the universe down to size—to make it humanly manageable. For instance, we usually accept that the Moon is big and far away, when it could easily be small and close by.'

'But triangulation——'

'With all due respect to Euclid and the gang, my second equation shows that triangulation is impossible, because there can't be any true angles.'

'All well and good,' said Kalendorf. 'But one day men will conquer the Moon. They'll build spaceships and land on it—in about A.D. 2120 or so—and then your second equation won't matter a damn.'

Porteus laughed. 'But don't you see, man? All their spaceships and all their calculations will simply be distorted by the demands of space! They may appear to travel a quarter of a million miles—in reality they will go a few feet!'

'An interesting theory, doctor. Let's ask my assistant, Bowler, what he thinks of it. Bowler? That's odd, he was here a minute ago.'

'Maybe,' suggested the physicist with a smile, 'he simply walked off the edge of the universe and vanished.'

They strolled outside and gazed up at the full moon. Kalendorf lit his pipe. 'Hmm. Distance not existing. A tempting theory, Porteus. But how would you go about proving it?'

'Like this!' The physicist reached up and plucked the full moon from the sky.

'Good heavens!'

'Ha ha ha—maybe now you'll stop scoffing at my "crazy" ideas, eh, Kalendorf? Ha ha ha!' Laughing strangely, he began to flip the Moon in the air, asking for 'heads or tails'.

Then he threw it to the unprepared Kalendorf. It slipped through his fingers and vanished from view in the sand.

The astronomer was horrified. 'Good heavens, what have you done?'

'Never mind.' Porteus took a sixpence from his pocket and pasted it among the stars. 'You chaps will be quite as happy exploring this, come A.D. 2120.'

Just then Bowler trudged up, out of breath. 'You wouldn't believe where I've been,' he said. 'I fell off——'

'Yes, so Dr Porteus has been telling me. He's just been demonstrating that space is not spatially—er—as roomy as we had thought. You know what this means to your professional standing, Bowler, if such a theory becomes generally known?'

The assistant nodded. Without a further word, the two fell upon their scientific colleague and strangled him.

'We'll bury the body in the desert, Bowler.'

'I've a better idea, sir. Let me throw it off the edge of the universe.'

'Good thinking. While you're gone, I'll search his hotel room and burn any notes. We must hide all traces of this terrible secret—forever!'

Forever? No, only until a desert urchin tries to spend the strange 'coin' he finds ... only until a numismatic expert gets a good look at the Sixpence ... and even now a waiter is studying the equations on the tablecloth, murmuring to himself:

'Then triangles *are* impossible, after all ... hmm ...'

Solar Shoe-Salesman
By Chipdip K. Kill

I

Stan Houseman, shoe-salesman, punched a cupee of Kaff from the kitchen and scanned the footlines of his morning newsper:

OLYMPIC FINALS AT CARMODY STADIUM
POLICE BREAK UP HATTONITE RIOT

The stock market report listed only two corporations—the two which had between them divided the world—North American Boot & Shoe (Nabs) and Eurasian Footwear. Nabs was up two points, Eurafoot down the same, inevitably. In this two-person, zero-sum game, one side could only profit at the expense of the other. *Like Karen and me*, he thought grimly.

The corner of his eye caught movement—the racing figure of an autistic child. When he looked right at it, it was gone.

Karen came into the kitchen.

'Let's not start anything, for God's sake,' he said.

'I'm getting a divorce, Stan. I'm seeing the lawster this afternoon.'

Suddenly the coffee-substitute tasted very bitter.

II

Ed Pagon gazed into the camera face of 'Mel', the robot interviewer for KHBT-TV. 'Somehow I feel this is more than just a game I'm playing here today,' he said. 'I think a lot more is at stake here today than the Olympics jacks championship.'

'Tell me, Ed,' said the robot, 'How does it feel, being the only male contestant in this jacks tournament?'

How do you think it feels? Like being castrated, he thought. Forcing a smile, he replied, 'Frankly, I've always thought of jacks as a man's game, Mel. It's an art as well as a sport, and men traditionally excell in the arts . . .'

When the interview was over, Ed went into his dressing-room to warm up. He seated himself on the floor with the regulation red rubber ball and steel jacks, and tried to empty his mind for Zen exercises. The idea was to pick up jacks without picking them up mentally.

Onesies without thinking about it. Twosies without thinking about it. Threesies . . .

Ed felt sudden pain, a band of it, squeezing his guts. Pain blurred his vision as he looked down at the jack on the floor. This was no jack. It was a tiny metal man with his arms outstretched, fastened by magnets to a steel cross.

III

Joe Feegle stopped Stan Houseman outside the sales cubicle. 'The word is, we're on the brink of war, Stan. The two company presidents are having a summit meeting this afternoon—they'll be playing one round of The Game—and if they tie, we'll have war.'

'But they always tie.'

'Right. Hey, look!'

Both men turned to stare at a figure at the other end of the corridor, a figure in the official gold-and-black uniform of an Armorer. President Moniter was calling in an Armorer to design new weapons for the company—a bad omen.

Another was the unrest caused, or exploited, by the barefoot fanatic sect who called themselves the Hattonites. As Stan unlocked his cubicle and prepared for work, he thought of Herkimer Hatton's strange and fascinating cult.

Little was known of the late Herkimer Hatton himself, except that he'd lived twenty years before, and had been accident-prone in the extreme. In a series of over a thousand small accidents, Hatton had lost limbs and other bits and pieces of his body, and replaced them with synthetics. Finally he was (except to his followers) an android. Legend had it that he'd finished up on an iron cross, and that he would return when the world needed him.

And now the world needed something, and fast. Stan cleared his mind of Hatton and other worries, and turned the energy of his psychic influence upon a million potential customers. His influence spread over the city, giving a million men and women this imperceptible nudge. For some it might come as a moment of reflection: *I do need new shoes* ... For others it might be a slight hesitation as they passed a Nabs window display. Still others would be in the stores, trying shoes on, when suddenly they'd find something ...

IV

Ferris Moniter, president of Nabs, glimpsed what looked like an autistic child out of the corner of his eye. He bumped his head as he stepped into his private autogyro.

'Ow. Second time I've bumped my head on that doorframe.'

His bodyguard, Truit, stiffened. 'Yes? Don't close that door just yet, sir. I want a look at that frame.' His expert fingers sought and found a tiny hairlike wire. 'Just as I thought, Mr Moniter. An animal magnet, set there to attract your head. Looks like the work of Nexus Brill.'

'Eurafoot's Armorer? But assassination's against the rules!'

The bodyguard laughed. 'Armorers have no rules, sir. My guess is, he meant to stun you, just before the Game. Probably had a side bet on it. They say Brill is rich from betting on the Game. Owns Paris, Rome, Antwerp, a dozen such cities. They say he's had some of them miniaturized and made into charms for his wife's charm bracelet. By the way, it might interest you to know that *our* Armorer, Amos Honks, visited the office this morning, while you were out. He may have had access to the autogyro ...'

Ferris Moniter blinked. 'You can't mean that, Truit! Why, Amos Honks is our only hope. Think of all the weaponry he's designed for us! How can you suspect him?'

Truit thought of the aerial battleship, filled with hydrogen and surrounded with heavy armor. 'I know, sir—but I can't help feeling that the two Armorers are in cahoots, somehow.'

Moniter sighed. 'Anyway, are there any more assassination attempts in the cards today?'

'Not *cards*, sir.' Truit sounded pained. '*Tiles*. Let's have a look.' He laid out the traditional tiles of the eleventh-century Chinese game of prophecy, *Mah-Jongg*. 'I'm afraid it's the

East Wind, sir. And the Four of Bamboos.'

'Oh? Is that bad? What's the reading?'

Truit opened the book and read:

'Many small greatnesses deny.
No same.
It does not further to discover several gifts only.
The wise king avoids fried foods.'

He closed the book. 'Sir, I think it's dangerous to continue this trip to Chicago.'

'Nonsense, Truit. I must go on. I must play and win. To give up now would mean economic collapse, the resurgence of the old, corrupt U.N., and slavery for most of the human race. The tiles must be wrong for once.'

But he knew the tiles were never wrong.

V

At Carmody stadium, the robot doctorator was examining Ed Pagon after his collapse. He lay on the dressing-room floor, doubled up with pain. The robot's probes moved to check his respiration, pulse, heart, temperature...

'What is it, doc?' asked an official. 'Appendicitis?'

The doctorator peered at him over its square-rimmed glasses. 'Don't quote me on this, boys,' it said, rubbing its iron chin. 'But it 'pears as if this here fella is fixing to have a baby!'

VI

Amos Honks, Armorer, awoke to a sense of danger. Karen Houseman was still asleep beside him.

He remembered the whole nightmarish episode at Nabs: Ferris Moniter telling him to arm the corporation for AOW, All-Out War. Ferris Moniter telling him he'd have to do better than hay-fever bombs, better even than *Herpes simplex*, the cold-sore virus, dropped in drinking water supplies.

'You'll have to do a lot better,' Moniter had said. 'Don't forget, you're up against Nexus Brill... by the way, did you know your wife's been seen with Brill?'

And later, she couldn't deny it. The world had come to a

sickening halt then, this afternoon at the lawster's office, when they obtained their punched card decree. There he'd met Karen Houseman, and the two new divorced people had just naturally clung together ... so here he was, still sensing danger like a smell of fear.

Outside he could hear the sound of muffled rotors—a police gyro trying to land quietly in the yard. He sensed, rather than heard, the faceless lawman creeping toward the house, the sound of a weapon being eased from its plastic holster and aimed through the wall at his brainwaves ... the trigger being squeezed ...

Amos rolled across the bed and hit the floor just as the humming green beam of a stupidifier flicked through the wall. It caught Karen and she slumped sideways, babbling and drooling.

Before the cop could fire again, Amos snatched a charm off his wife's charm bracelet, flung open the door and pitched it into the yard. It was a miniaturized city. He counted to ten and breathed, 'Goodbye, Paris.'

With a thunder of cobblestones, the minicity sprang to full size in the yard. He heard the cop's scream, cut off by a shriek of tires and the blare of a taxi horn.

Amos smashed a window, gashing his arm, and raced across the Place de la Bastille to the empty police autogyro. He climbed in, took off and headed for Chicago. There had to be some way to stop the Game—before the Game stopped everything else.

If only he could design some weapon Nexus Brill could not counter. He played the stream of ideas across the porcelain surfaces of his mind:

How about mad dogs? A nullitron beam? Unconscious mines? Fire-cabbages ... even an Earth-mover, which could shift the entire planet during an aerial battle, thus leaving enemy aircraft stranded in outer space.

Why was it Nexus Brill always had his ideas first? As he wondered, the aura began. The perimeter of his vision was filled with autistic children; his ears jangled with flashing lightmares, and he felt the deep molecular and genetic shift begin.

He was, as usual, turning into Nexus Brill.

VII

The autistic child pointed to a picture of Stan Houseman and said, 'Nice mans.'

The Hattonite elders looked at one another. Why 'mans'? Could Houseman be, after all, the discalced prophet promised by Herkimer Hatton?

VIII

The data-scan footline flickered upon the instrument panel of the autogyro:

LABORS OF HERCULES?
Athlete to give birth!

'I don't understand that,' said Ferris Moniter, looking away to the still blue waters of the Americ Ocean. An hour remained before they reached the finger-shaped Isle of Michigan, with Chicago glittering at its tip like a bright hangnail. Far to the east lay the dark continent of Atlantica, broken only by the British Lakes; beyond that, the Europic Sea.

'In this novel I'm reading,' he said, taking the foilback from his pockette, 'the author pretends that Lucifer *lost* his war against Heaven, so that all the world is reversed, see?'

Truit, his bodyguard, laughed. 'Science fiction eh? Don't believe everything you see in white on black. What's the name of this book?'

'Autogyro Ace,' said the president. 'An Autogyro Novel, by Killhip D. Pick.'

At that moment a dot appeared above the horizon, far behind them. It grew rapidly to another autogyro.

'Who is it, Truit?'

'Too far to see, sir. Might be friendly...' The bodyguard trained his electric binoculars on the strange craft, then gasped. 'No! It can't be!'

In a moment the stranger was close enough for Moniter to

see, too. *The other autogyro contained another Ferris Moniter and another Truit.* As he watched, it came closer, passed through his own craft and sped on toward Chicago.

IX

The president of Eurafoot sat in shadow behind the Game table, a masked entity without a name.

'Sit you down, Mr Moniter,' said a disembodied voice. 'You know the rules of the Game.' When Truit had checked the seat for bombs and virus, Moniter took his place. An aide brought in a pad of paper and ruled the traditional four lines on its top sheet: Two horizontal, two vertical.

'You may go first, Mr Moniter. You have "X", and the advantage—for the moment.'

From the next room came gunshots and electric fizzling, as Eurafoot's androids joined with Nabs's cyborgs to fight off Hattonite assassins.

As Moniter started to make his move, his opponent leaned forward, bringing his face into the light.

'You!'

X

Joe Feegle wrote, 'It was a two-person, zero-sum game. Stan Houseman had established that general strict determinateness held in all cases of special strict determinateness, and in other cases as well, but he had not excluded the possibility that the advance from special to general determinateness was no advance at all! Then he himself was an android, too!'

Joe was working on his novel, ANDROGYNOID, written under the pseudonym 'H. K. (Kid) Cliplip'. Joe suffered from the delusion that he himself was written, under a pseudonym.

XI

'You see,' said the president of Eurafoot, 'when Nexus Brill broke that window, he cut himself. He is now infected with a virus that will scourge our planet. It causes the feet to rot off, heh heh.'

'I think Amos Honks will have something to say about that,'

said a voice from the dark doorway.

'The autistic child!'

'Wrong,' said Stan Houseman. He fired the demoralizer beam once, and the odd president flopped, spineless, to the floor. It was the end of the universe, all agreed.

XII

Nexus Brill saw the great ruled line coming across the sky. He speeded up the autogyro and tried to take evasive action, but it was no use. The ruled line reached him and cut him, along with the earth and sky, clean in two.

XIV

'So it was Ed Pagon who gave birth to the new universe, eh?'

'Right. There weren't really any sides, since each company owned all the stock of the other, anyway. And since both were really owned by the Hattonites . . .'

'Then everyone was an android, really.'

'Brill must have suspected as much. When he cut himself on that window, he failed to bleed.'

He shook his head. 'Brill *was* human, though bloodless.'

She smiled. 'Then . . . it's all over?'

'In a sense.'

So saying, Stan and Karen Houseman walked barefoot with the other pilgrims, into the former shoestore.

Floogy Flarl was a wipeout man
Cashed his cogs, that wipeout man
Nobody knew how it all began
But Floogy Flarl

The Co-ordainer's name was Hampton Syzygy of the planet Chicago, and he longed to go home. Even though he had to travel far beyond the Asteroid River of Mkaj, far beyond the Gaderene Galaxies and even to the edge of Edgeitself itself, his heart was turning ever homeward, toward the old Folkstad Ohm. But when his heart turned toward Folkstad Ohm it was full of bitterness and revenge, for Ohm was the ancient Lord of the Facility who had inherited Chicago, inherited it by killing former owner, the tyrant Stulk Hermanø. Ohm had ended Hermanø's reign of blood only to begin his own. There was a song about this, too:

Stulk was wrong, but he wronged the wrong
While Folkstad wronged the right.

Hampton would soon do something about Folkstad Ohm, just as he would later undergo seven trials on the seven planets of Smurr. He would do these things that the adventure books might be filled with stories. But the adventure books came later, and Hampton Syzygy knew nothing of them, for he lived in the present. There was a song about this, too, but now is not for songs, but stories. And of all stories, the most strange and wonderful is the story of how Hampton Syzygy came home to Chicago, and why.

Hampton came back to Chicago by way of an otherfolk planet, Marvin Jarvis. The people of Marvin Jarvis were all otherfolk, created from animals to serve the human race and the Lords of the Facility. Two guides met Hampton at the spaceport: a sly-looking couple named F'Red and F'Annie, with their little son, F'art.

'We're not completely human,' F'Red said. 'We're really cleverly mutated foxes. That is, I am a fox, and F'Annie is a vixen. I forget whether F'art is called a pup or a cub.' After failing to sell Hampton a used car, the couple drifted away in the crowd of otherfolk.

There were all kinds here: B'Ernie, the beaverman who built dams; E'Laine, the elephantgirl with the phenomenal memory; P'Rick, the porcupineman, a deadly archer. Of course there were ostrichfolk hiding their heads in the sand; swanfolk who could break a human's arm with one stroke of a powerful wing; snakemen who hypnotized (though their chief victims were birdfolk); electric eelmen working at the power station and many more. Hampton strolled through the streets, nodding and smiling to animalfolk friends. B'Ill the batman was trying to entangle himself in a womanman's hair. B'Ill the bearman seemed hungry enough to eat a horseman. B'Ill the budgieman and W'Rita the wormgirl dropped their tasks and followed at Hampton's command.

It was here that Hampton met M'Arlene, who taught him subtle and peculiar ways. He would not be able to take M'Arlene with him when he left Marvin Jarvis planet. She knew that and accepted it, and yet she ached to go with him, along with W'Rita and B'Ill. But they could help Hampton Syzygy, and M'Arlene could not.

There was nothing on Chicago that a monkeywoman could do.

Before he reached Chicago, Hampton Syzygy had to spend a year being scent-cleared on the planet Kipling Glory. The police agents of Chicago were dog-robots, trained to detect the smell of any out-planet on a man, be it eleven months old. This was the only out-planet where a man could acquire a new, acceptable smell.

Kipling Glory was a skull, the skull of the ancient giant Johow, slaughtered, it was said, by the Montag brothers. They had made of his spine a great starship capable of 'light-doubling' itself across the universe, and they had set out to find the Center of the Pattern. Living here on a giant skull reminded Hampton of what Folkstad Ohm had done to the Syzygy family, and his thoughts were cold-tinged with the feel of revenge.

The day for revenge must come, but now it was time for waiting and for watching, and for washing the dishes. Disguised in the body of an idiot dishwasher, Hampton waited and watched and worked. The dirty dishes came in to the steamy yellow kitchen. Hampton breathed upon them, reaching down inside each dish with his mind and making it *wish* to be clean, making it vibrate with the hope of cleanliness. Dishwishing, he called it, and worked at it for eleven months and more, until it was time to throw off his disguise and come to Chicago.

On Chicago he first visited, almost without realizing where he was going, the Shrine of the Seventh Type of Ambiguity. It stood on a hill overlooking the Desert of Doris Deadlock, an old computer set in the ruins of what once had been the English department of a university, when men had studied English as a medical and legal language. This old computer had long been used by the otherfolk as an oracle.

'Why do we come to this place, O Human?' said W'Rita. 'You do not believe in the power of the oracle.'

'I do not disbelieve, either. Anyway, this place is sacred to my family. It was near here my father, Herman Syzygy fought the Last Light-Swallower and killed it, and for that they made him a Protector of the Check.'

W'Rita smiled, insofar as a worm can be said to smile. 'That is true. What will you ask the oracle?'

But Hampton could not answer, for he would not allow himself to think of a question in advance. That way the computer's telepathic capabilities would become as nothing, and he might gain power over it.

The question he finally did ask, standing on the windswept bluff overlooking the Venn Diagram Lakes, was:

'What has one leg in the morning, four legs in the afternoon and three legs in the evening, and when is a door not a door?'

'Hmmm,' said the old computer. 'That's a toughy. Would it be Long John Silver with a three-legged parrot?'

'No.'

'How about a leg of mutton magically transformed into a dog that pees on your doorstep at dusk?'

'No.'

'Okay, I give. What is it?'

'A coffee table, made from a door!' Hampton explained how one began in the morning by putting one leg on, and then had all four in place by the afternoon, but one fell off in the evening. The old computer gave him a secret whereby he might ensnare the tyrant Ohm. W'Rita, the wormgirl who had been bred and created to tie packages up real pretty, now tied herself around Hampton's finger so he would not forget the secret. They descended and began to cross the Desert of Doris Deadlock.

They made the crossing at night, when the sand was cool and blue-gray, and the sagebrush silver in the moonlight. Now and then Hampton glimpsed the desert's owner, Doris herself, flitting behind a rock or bush. He knew it was truly Doris, for the moonlight gleamed on the padlock through her nose.

At dawn Hampton entered the capital city Vb and went straight to the palace of Folkstad Ohm. On the way, he explained to B'Ill the budgieman why he was needed.

'Like all budgiemen, you were bred and created to guard mirrors, and that is what you must do now. I want you to guard all mirrors at the palace against the false image of Folkstad Ohm; otherwise he may slip in among his false images and escape my revenge. Do you understand?'

'I understand and obey, O Human,' said the budgieman, and seeing that the occasion was serious, he forbore adding the 'Who's a pretty boy?' that was at the tip of his tongue. Hampton entered the palace the way M'Arlene had showed him, and made his way to the private chambers of the tyrant.

'I've been expecting you,' said Ohm, looking up from his clairevoyance machine. Suddenly he made a dash at a mirror on the nearest wall, trying to slip into his false image, but B'Ill was there before him.

Now Folkstad Ohm turned craven. 'What do you want of me, Syzygy? I can't bring your wife and children back to life, can I?'

Revenge clouded Hampton's mind, as he raised a death-weapon to spill the tyrant's blood. Ohm had done a terrible thing to Mrs Syzygy and the children, by changing their spaceness. Hampton's wife had been shrunk to the size of a dust mote, and battered to death by the Brownian motion in a sunbeam. The oldest of his two children had been made to swell to such a size that gravity collapsed his bones. He was now the Ricky Syzygy mountain range. Little Lydia, the baby, had been neither shrunk nor grown, but made so heavy that she sank to the molten center of the planet and became one with it. Hampton thought of her every time he felt the tug of gravity. Revenge clouded his mind and he raised his weapon.

But then he saw W'Rita tied to his finger, and remembered the secret of the old computer. Reaching down inside the future, Hampton made some adjustments. This event became contingent upon that and the other, while another event vanished for good. As he worked, he spoke to Folkstad Ohm.

'Whatever you hurt, you will be. Whatever you hate will be you. All your daggers backwards turn. O-U-T spells out goes he, with a dirty dishrag on his knee.'

Disbelieving in the spell, Ohm tried kicking a passing dog. In the instant before it felt the crushing pain of his iron boot against its ribs, the dog and Ohm exchanged consciousness. As a dog, he felt the ribs crack, and hot electric pain shot through him. He tried to bite the tyrant leg, and found himself back in his own body to be savaged by a pain crazed animal. The sentence was eternal, and just.

Hampton Syzygy returned to his own home, where he lived in peace for many years, until he fell asleep and went to hunt with his ancestors. But high above the Venn Diagram Lakes, the old computer still chuckled to himself, for the sixty or seventy millionth time:

'A coffee table! Well I'll be damned!'

The Sublimation World
By J. G. B——

Chapter I: The Eternal Grocer

Price looked across the lagoon, a dry sweep of land, at the mirage. The lagoon was sublimating, turning from liquid ice directly into crystalline air, and through its wavering layers he could make out a Giacometti statue that was probably one of King's men, grown thin. Fronds of zygote enwrapped the old supermarket now, smothering it in lianas and spermaceti, turning it into a fairly good Jackson Pollock painting, the one he always dreamed about. This, too, had a dreamlike mist about it, as did King's man, turning and turning, driven by a wind of solidity. Pterodactyls honked overhead.

Chapter II: The Harpies' Bazaar

It had become more than a month between Price's visits to the kayak. Mona lay back in the kayak in her yellow empire gown, trailing one lavender glove in the water. Pterodactyls watched as she combed and brushed out her hair, using for a mirror a smoothed slab of the atmosphere. Price felt suddenly very tired—but then he had always been suddenly tired. He wanted to give it all up, to sublimate awhile with the world around him, to rise beating leathern wings into the hot purple sunset. But this could not be, not for the moment. He still felt a peculiar loyalty to the human species. There was still the scurvy to be cleared up, the report to write, the generator to be fixed. He lit his pipe and frowned through its azure smoke at King's elephant. It was marching about in a circle, waving a black flag.

Chapter III: Mirror of Xanadu

He would write to the government he thought, coming out of the dream. It was always the same—a hollow, hot, heavy jungle tree, bright green, growing right in the middle of a frozen desert amid yellow orange flames and bearing seven blue grapes. He picked them, one at a time, and crushed them between his toes. The juice ran like blood into the parched flank of earth. But the last grape he reserved, to crush against the roof of his mouth like a spy's poison capsule, before he died. In the dream he never died.

Chapter IV: Desert of Gas

Man has caused the sublimation. For years, decades, man had poured black, oily fumes into the atmosphere. Some of these fumes descended as solids, to soak into the earth once more, to polarize its proteins. Other matter had risen, faster during the warm days and slower at night, until it reached the sun, altering it slowly and subtly. For over a hundred years, the sun had been getting dirty; now its purplish glow turned the sensitive proteins of earth into iodine.

Price lived in a small, abandoned Abbey, sleeping on the altar and using the decaying harmonium for a cupboard. He kept in the cupboard a few time-fragments, relics of his own past: a bead belt he'd made in scouts; a rusted mouse; a stamped, self-addressed anvelope; a bottle of hair-oil that he kept despite his baldness. It was *oil*, after all, sacred chrism, and things in the Jurassic past had died to create it . . .

A shot echoed across the iodine flats. One of Mona's kites fluttered like an angry angel's wing, flickered across his vision and fell. In the distance, Joe Olifant had wrapped himself in a black mantle. He drove madly about in his chariot, his whip flickering out like the tongue of a lizard. Price could hear the frightened screams of the horses and Joe's dark, Rasputin laugh.

Chapter V: The Parsee of the Cobra Casino

King had in his great circus train more food and water and treasure than he and his assassins could hope to use up. It was foolish of Price to try holding out against them. They were the cruel life-force itself. Why should he drink dew? Why cook his last tins of food over a fire of pterodactyl guana? There was finally nothing left to eat but his beaded belt and the few peanuts that King's sharp-eyed elephant might overlook.

King had parked his train in a circle, broken only where the chip of blue lake lay soundless, mirroring nightly strange rites. By the light of gas torches, the tattooed woman was charming a cobra. King lay, in his red silk mandarin pajamas, on an enamelled couch, fanning himself with one of Mona's kites. He was barely visible, a slash of red among the yellow balloons, like a wound. At his feet, the pet pterodactyl was busy, methodically ripping apart a peacock.

Chapter VI: An Ozymandian Tangram

There was no water anywhere. All the water had grown heavy and sunk out of sight beneath the earth, which was slowly turning to dry ice. At last Price hitched up the remains of his belt—so emaciated was he become that, though he had eaten half of it, the belt still fit him—and struck out for the purple flats. *I must look like a Giacometti,* he thought. The silver flats turned azure-gray at noon, while the heated air became dank and brown. He looked back and saw the galloping skeleton of the elephant, the howda swaying. King, or the ghost of King, was pursuing him, a ghost. They couldn't let him go off and die alone. They wanted to punish him for turning his back on them, for refusing, like some inverse Toby Tyler, to join their circus.

The elephant was dissolving, and King, sinking slowly to the ground, was falling behind. He took up the electric megaphone and shouted:

'Come back Price. We need you at camp. Don't be a bloody fool, man!'

Chapter VII: The Bloody Fool

He came upon the dead city at dusk. For awhile he was apprehensive that King might pursue him here, too, using the circus train. Then he saw that the railroad had long since vaporized, leaving only an ash of tracks. The station, too, was a ghost. He had reached the end of the line, the terminal terminal. The whole city was a gibbous dune, once a mercury refinery, now frozen into a single gaseous crystalline chrysalid, depended from what was once a flaming bloodfruit tree, now gone to iron, ironically.

The tree reminded him of something. He took out the blue grape to eat and found that it, too, was diminished, worn away by the invisible though solid wind that moved from past to future.

Other Panthers For Your Enjoyment

Science Fiction and Fantasy

☐ **H. P. Lovecraft** **AT THE MOUNTAINS OF MADNESS** **25p**
A great collection of sinister and uncanny tales for connoisseurs of terror.

☐ **H. P. Lovecraft** **THE CASE OF CHARLES DEXTER WARD** **25p**
A short macabre novel by the 20th century's undisputed master of horror.

☐ **Keith Roberts** **PAVANE** **30p**
An alternative universe in which 20th century England is still under the grimly reactionary rule of the Roman Church.
'His blend of telling detail, gripping story line and pure exalted fantasy is little short of miraculous' – *Tribune*. 'Brilliant' – *SF Review*

☐ **Roger Zelazny** **LORD OF LIGHT** **40p**
'A triumph' said the *Magazine of Fantasy and Science Fiction*. 'A rare work of SF imagination' added the *Sunday Telegraph*. And the final accolade – the Hugo Award. In an era yet to come and a planet far distant from this one a group of way-out men and women, backed by a powerful technology that makes ours look primitive, take over the role of the ancient Hindu pantheon.

☐ **Roger Zelazny** **THE DREAM MASTER** **25p**
A mind-stretching story of a lonely voyager's nightmare journey into the infinity of inner space. By a master of contemporary SF.

☐ **John Blackburn** **CHILDREN OF THE NIGHT** **30p**
A pothole on the Yorkshire moors and an ancient race emerging from it to once more – after eons of time – take its 'rightful' place on Earth's surface – 'rightfully' meaning that humans go to the wall. One of the eeriest thrillers published in years. John Blackburn is streets ahead of all his competitors in this field.